I0771614

Scout

Book 1

SAMANTHA COLE

To Joseph Mortimer Granville (1833-1900), the inventor of the electromechanical vibrator.

One

Scout Turner sighed in annoyance as he closed a file and added it to the rejection pile on his desk. He needed a new personal assistant, and not a single candidate out of twenty-two impressed him. Well, that wasn't true. Alex Shepherd was ideal on paper, and Scout had looked forward to seeing if he made the same impression when they met in person. But Shepherd hadn't shown up for his interview, which had been scheduled to start ten minutes ago. Tardiness was something Scout refused to allow in his employees unless there was a damn good reason for it. He hadn't created a business empire by accommodating other people's shortcomings. So, Shepherd's file got tossed on top of the others, which would be shredded in the near future. If the man couldn't attend the initial job interview on time, how could Scout expect anything more from him?

It was two weeks since he fired Erik Fisher, his PA for the past thirty months, after finding out he was resentful of the men Scout saw socially. He'd screwed around with his boss's schedule, emails, and phone messages, deleting some and switching the times on others. Scout missed several dates over the past six or eight months and wondered why a few of the guys he'd been into suddenly stopped making contact.

Apparently, Erik wanted much more from his employer than just a paycheck. Scout made it a habit not to date anyone who worked for him or had business dealings with him, not that he was attracted to Erik at all anyway. Yes, he was good-looking, in a metro-sexual kind of way, but Scout hadn't experienced any interest in the man on a personal level since the day he was hired. When he discovered what Erik had been up to, sabotaging his private life, Scout canned him on the spot and banned him from all his properties. And now, when he should concentrate on the new hotel he was building in Seattle, among other things, Scout was stuck without a PA until he found one who suited him.

As president and CEO of Turner Continental, Scout owned several hotels, including the one he used as his home base—the Paradox Hotel & Residencies in San Francisco. The other hotels and a few restaurants, clubs, and condo complexes were in various cities up and down the West Coast. One of his newest ventures, in which he agreed to be a silent partner, was the Cock & Bull, a pub that recently opened directly across the street from the Paradox. His longtime friend, Rico Demara, was the primary owner and manager. Scout looked forward to watching the man succeed—and not just from a financial standpoint either. The profits Scout expected from the C & B didn't come close to those of his other properties. But Rico overcame a lot since his teens, and it was about time the guy was involved in something positive for a change.

"I'm sorry, Mr. Shepherd." Delilah Webb's no-nonsense voice filtered through the slightly open door separating his office from hers. She was Scout's secretary for the past ten years, watching his company grow from a single renovated hotel to its conglomerate status, and she guarded him like a pit bull. More than once, he'd asked her to change positions and be his PA, but she turned him down each time, saying she was quite comfortable with her current job. The PA's position also required a lot of travel and after-hours meetings and events, and Delilah preferred to spend that time with her husband, children, and grandchildren. "Your appointment was fifteen minutes ago. You were marked as a no-show, and there are no second chances with Mr. Turner. You should have called."

"But, please. I really need this job. I didn't mean to be late—" The rich, baritone voice caught Scout's attention. Something about it sent a delicious shiver down his spine. He brought his computer out of sleep mode and clicked on the program connected to the hotel's security feeds. He quickly found the one for Delilah's office and studied the man standing in front of her desk. Shepherd gave the phrase tall, dark, and handsome a new and intriguing meaning.

"And yet you are."

"I know, and I'm really sorry. It was unavoidable. Please. Is there any chance I can reschedule?" Through the camera lens, Scout could see genuine dejection and dismay on the man's face, along with a chiseled jaw and slightly crooked nose as if it'd been broken once before.

From Shepherd's job application and résumé, Scout knew he was thirty-four and had a bachelor's degree in hospitality management and an associate's degree in business administration from New York University. Following that, he had an impressive career at the Four Seasons Hotel in New York City, climbing the ranks until he became a junior executive. He recently relocated to California for undisclosed family reasons, and Scout was suddenly curious about what they were. While he could be a bitch of a boss to work for, he did have a heart when it came to the faithful employees of Turner Continental. Delilah and the managers of each of his properties kept him up to date on things like deaths, births, marriages, etc., in the families of his employees. He made sure Delilah sent each one an appropriate card and gift from him. His father had done it for years in his own real estate investment company, and Scout continued the tradition.

Delilah shook her head. "The best I can do is to pass along your request to Mr. Turner, but honestly, I don't expect him to relent and give you another chance. The man runs a tight ship. He demands the best from his employees, who respect him enough to give it to him."

Letting out a heavy breath, Shepherd nodded his head in resignation. "I understand that, but I'd appreciate it if he could give me another chance to prove myself. That's all I'm asking for."

"I'll see that he gets the message."

He glanced around before nodding again. "Thank you."

Scout watched the man's shoulders slump as he turned around and strode out the door. Delilah was right. He rarely gave second chances, but a part of him wanted to offer Shepherd one—and he had no clue why.

After shutting down his computer, he picked up the stack of personnel files and made sure he had his phone and keys before heading to the outer office. Delilah looked up at him as he approached, then grinned and shook her head. "I'm still not used to you without the facial hair. You startle me every time I see you."

"Startles me every time I look in the mirror too." Two nights ago, he'd lost a bet with a friend and had to shave off the beard and mustache he sported for the past twelve years. While he always kept them short and neat, suddenly having bare skin on his face was disconcerting. His jaw and upper lip seemed ultra-sensitive to heat and cold since he had lost the extra layer of protection, and it was a shock when he touched his face after forgetting the coarse hair was gone. Unfortunately, the bet also required him not to let the stubble grow back for one month, so he was stuck with shaving every freaking day, something he didn't look forward to. Regardless of how much it sucked, Scout wasn't one to renege on a bet or a deal he'd shaken on. But in the future, all wagers that required him to lose any hair on his body were out.

Delilah took the files from him and raised her eyebrows when he snatched the top one back. The wise woman hadn't missed the name on the front of the folder. "You heard he showed up late?"

"Yup."

"He'd like to reschedule."

"So he said." Scout had no idea why he was even contemplating giving the man the second chance he'd begged for, but he wouldn't make any rash decisions. "I'll think about it. He *was* the most qualified of all the applicants, at least on paper."

She held out her hand. "I'll put it back on your desk. Let me know if you want me to call him for another interview."

After passing the file to her, he asked, "Anything else I need to know about before I leave?"

"Not a thing. I'll see you tomorrow. Have a good evening."

"You—"

His automatic response was cut short by the phone ringing on Delilah's desk. He waited a moment while she answered to ensure nothing that needed his attention had come up before he went home to unwind for the night.

"Yes, Phillipe, he's still here." She glanced up at him as she spoke to the maître d' of the hotel's five-star restaurant, Sapphire's. "Okay, I'll let him know." She hung up the phone. "The mayor, his wife, and two guests just walked in for dinner. Phillipe thought you might want to swing by and say hello."

"Personally? No. Professionally . . ." He rolled his eyes, which caused her to laugh. Scout hated politics more than anything in the world, but concessions had to be made at times to succeed in a business like his. "After I play nice with the mayor and his guests, I'll call it a night. See you tomorrow."

It wasn't as if he had a long way to go to get home at the end of the day. His place was one of two penthouse residences in the building. The first three levels were where all the amenities were located, including Sapphire's, a separate bar, the Ivy Bistro—which served breakfast and lunch—conference rooms, a gym, ballrooms, etc. All the business offices, including Scout's, were on the fourth floor. The next twenty-four floors were guest rooms and suites. Above them were another twelve floors, each with four condos. The owners of those units had their own parking garage, storage space, entrance, and elevators. They also had access to all the hotel's facilities, which were included in their common charges if they wanted to use them. Each 2,000-square-foot condo had started with a base price of $700,000 while the place was being built, and they sold out within two months. The timing allowed buyers to customize their kitchens, bathrooms, and flooring with upgrades, which most had done. One of the original owners recently sold his condo for a very nice profit at $1.3 million.

The penthouse level was the highest point, with only two 4,000-square-foot units, one of which Scout lived in.

After stopping in the men's lavatory and checking his appearance, Scout took the stairs to the lobby instead of riding the elevator down. On the weekends, Scout wore a polo shirt with the Paradox or Turner Continental logo and a pair of dress pants. During the week, however, he always wore a suit. He was fond of designer clothes and loved it when a suit was custom-made for his six-foot, two-hundred-pound, muscular frame.

As he strode through the lobby and into the restaurant, Scout's gaze took in his surroundings, ensuring everything was how it was supposed to be and everyone appeared content. He was a stickler for detail, and his staff was trained to be the same way. The satisfaction of his guests and tenants was his number one priority. Happy guests will return and recommend the hotel to their friends and family.

It took a minute for Scout to realize most of his staff didn't recognize him. A few had done double-takes when he nodded and said hello to them before recognition kicked in. It was his first time being on the main floor since he lost the bet, and none of his employees had ever seen him clean-shaven before, except for two of his vice presidents who'd known him since college.

Stopping at the hostess stand, Scout waited for the attractive, leggy, blonde woman, manning the phones and greeting patrons at the door, to finish taking a reservation. As required, she wore a black dress that was neither too suggestive nor casual. After hanging up the phone, she gave him a brilliant smile and her full attention. "How may I help you, s—" Her blue eyes, enhanced with subtle makeup, widened. "Oh, Mr. Turner, I'm so sorry. I didn't recognize you."

He lifted his hand up in a reassuring gesture. "It's okay, Rebecca. You're not the only one. Don't get too used to it, though. I lost a bet and will grow it back next month."

A light laugh erupted from her. Like many Paradox's employees, she'd worked there for several years and learned to relax around the big boss while remaining professional. "Well, you still look very handsome, sir . . . different but handsome. Are you here for dinner?"

"No, Phillipe called and said the mayor was here with some guests."

"Yes, sir. They're at table twenty." When he raised his eyebrows at the mention of the second-best table in Sapphire's, she quickly explained, "Magnus Keller reserved table twenty-one for this evening and is due in about twenty minutes but said he might be a little late."

"Ah, okay. That's fine." Mag was one of the highest-paid actors in Hollywood for the past seven or eight years and a good friend of Scout's. He also owned the other penthouse in the Paradox. Either the man planned to entertain a date tonight, or a movie producer would try to schmooze him into starring in his or her next film. Those were the only times Mag used his status to request the best table in the house. Otherwise, he took what was available. However, the staff always took good care of him, no matter what, because of his celebrity status, his friendship with Scout, and the fact that he tipped very generously.

After spending a few minutes talking with the mayor and his party and politely declining an invitation to some political function, Scout made a point to stop by each occupied table, ensuring they had everything they needed. It was still early on a Wednesday evening, so the restaurant wasn't filled to capacity yet, but within an hour, it would be. Sapphire's head chef and staff had developed a considerable following since the place opened, and they rarely experienced a slow night.

After doing his duties and asking Rebecca to have someone bring the night's beef special to his penthouse in about an hour, Scout headed back into the lobby toward the elevators. He looked forward to getting out of his suit and into a pair of sweatpants and a T-shirt. A new James Rollins thriller waited for him on his coffee table, and reading it was his only plan for the next few hours. He was what his mother called an introverted extrovert. While he loved socializing occasionally, he would rather be on his own, kicking back and reading or watching TV a few nights a week. He enjoyed the solitude and quiet. Some guys he dated in the past had understood that and either joined him in a peaceful evening or left him alone. Others, though, couldn't understand why a wealthy man, who could afford to do anything he wanted in his spare time, would prefer to spend it behind closed doors instead of partying every night. Those guys rarely reached boyfriend status, as Scout ended things quickly when it became evident they only dated him for his money and social status.

As he was about to pass the hotel's lobby bar, a man sitting on a stool with his back to Scout caught his eye. A glance in the mirrored wall behind the rows of alcohol confirmed his suspicion. After a moment's hesitation, Scout altered his course, approached the bar, and took a seat beside Alex Shepherd. The man barely acknowledged him before returning his attention to the chilled, full glass of beer in front of him.

Scout ordered a club soda with lime from the bartender, who also didn't recognize him, and thanked him when it was promptly delivered. He suddenly realized his lack of facial hair allowed him to observe some of his employees and guests without being identified. He sat in silence for a few moments, studying the reflection of the man beside him in the mirror. He took in Shepherd's recently shaven jaw, dark eyes, brown hair with hints of red highlights, and kissable lips. The man was very striking and clearly still depressed about missing his interview.

Scout didn't know the name of the cologne Shepherd wore, but whatever the brand, it was damn enticing. Unable to resist, he sipped his drink and then asked, "Rough day?"

Shepherd spared him a brief glance before eyeing his beer again. "Yup. Lost out on the job I really wanted."

"That sucks. What happened?"

A loud sigh proceeded his answer. "It was my own damn fault. I was late to the interview and got blocked by the guy's secretary guarding his door. All because of a dog that got hit by a car."

Scout's eyes narrowed at the odd revelation. "A

dog? What does that have to do with you missing an interview? Did you hit it?"

"No! No. The ass that did kept going. I stopped. No one was around, and the dog didn't have a collar on. She was hurt pretty badly. I keep a blanket in the trunk of my car, so I used that to scoop her up and rush her to the closest vet I could find on Google. That's why I was late getting to the interview. I wanted to call on my way here to say I was running a few minutes late, but somewhere in that mess, I lost my phone. It's definitely not in my car because the Bluetooth wasn't picking it up. I called the vet's office from one of the house phones in the lobby, and they don't have it, so I probably dropped it on the road, and it's been smashed by a semi by now."

Of all the things the man could've said, rescuing a dog was the last excuse Scout expected. His gaze remained on the Shepherd's reflection, looking for any signs he recognized the owner of the Paradox and was trying to snow him. However, nothing but disappointment showed on Shepherd's face.

Scout's impression of the man shot up a few more points. "Is the dog going to be okay?"

"Yeah, the vet seems to think so. I asked when I called about my phone—she's got a broken leg and some bruising and road rash. They'll keep her for another day or two. It'll cost me over a grand to have her fixed up. From the condition she was in, even before the car hit her, it's obvious she's a stray. If I didn't agree to pay the vet bill, they would've put her down—humanely, of course."

His disgusted snort said he didn't think there was anything humane about euthanizing a dog simply because it was homeless. Scout silently agreed with him.

"Wow. That really sucks."

"Tell me about it. I can't let them kill her, and my apartment building doesn't allow pets, so somehow, I'll have to find a home for her before they release her. On top of all that, I need to get a new phone now and start looking for a job again."

"What happened to your old one? Your job, I mean. I assume you had one." Of course, Scout knew that from the man's résumé.

"Yeah. One I really liked, but my mom had a mild stroke two months ago. She's okay but needs to use a walker now. My dad and sister can easily care for her with the help of a home health aide, but I couldn't sit back in New York and let them deal with everything here." He shrugged as if the decision had been a no-brainer. "So, I gave a month's notice and moved back to the Bay Area to do whatever I could to help my family."

"Just like that? Without having another job lined up?"

"I thought I *did* have one. Three days before I was supposed to start, the hotel announced it was being sold in a merger, and all personnel decisions were put on hold until further notice. Even though I was offered the job, I hadn't started yet, so . . ." He shrugged instead of finishing the sentence.

Scout knew precisely which hotel Shepherd was referring to. He considered an attempt to acquire the property, but after getting a consultant's report, he decided against it.

Shepherd had a massive heart to go with his impressive résumé. Scout didn't know many people who would willingly be late to an interview with him to save a dog's life. Shepherd also left a job he loved to be near his parents and sister. Family was important to Scout—he was very close to his—and Turner Continental was an extension of that. Alex Shepherd was the type of man who would fit right in with the company.

With a decision made, Scout pulled his wallet out of his pants pocket and tossed a twenty next to his soda, indicating to the bartender he would also pay for the other man's drink. He then retrieved a business card and dropped it in front of Shepherd. "Call my secretary in the morning and reschedule the interview for tomorrow afternoon. I rarely give second chances, so don't be late this time."

He almost laughed out loud as Shepherd's eyes nearly bugged out of their sockets when he read the card and then stared at him in disbelief. "You're— you're Scout Turner?"

He smirked. "Minus the beard and mustache, yeah, I'm him. See you tomorrow." He started to turn away but then paused. "Bring the dog's vet bill with you. I'll take care of it."

If Shepherd's jaw dropped any further, it would've hit the bar. "Mr. Turner, I-I don't know what—"

"Just be on time," he reminded him again. Without letting the man get another word in, Scout left him in shock. If Shepherd arrived early for his interview, as Scout expected, he'd certainly get the job.

<h1 style="text-align:center">Two</h1>

Riding the elevator up to the fourth floor, in a repeat of yesterday, minus the injured dog and with a new cell phone, Alex checked his tie in the mirrored door. He then wiped his sweaty palms on his ass, under his jacket, where any moisture wouldn't be noticed, and willed his hammering heart to slow down a bit. It was years since he'd been to a job interview, and he hoped this would be the last one for a long time. How he got so lucky to run into Scout Turner in the bar yesterday was beyond him, but he wouldn't look a gift horse in the mouth.

Alex immediately noticed the good-looking man who had sat beside him the previous day but was too annoyed about the missed opportunity to engage him in conversation. Then, the man turned the tables on him. In preparing for yesterday's interview, Alex studied everything he could find about Scout Turner, looking for ways to make a good impression. Still, he hadn't discovered any recent photos of him without the beard and mustache. Hence, he hadn't realized that the owner of Turner Continental was the same man he'd discreetly ogled as they talked.

As the elevator doors slid open, he checked his watch for the eighth or ninth time since entering the lobby a few minutes ago. It was ten to three—early enough, but not too much as to seem overly eager. Not that it mattered. Turner knew Alex desperately wanted the job—he said as much in the bar before knowing who the man was.

He approached the impeccably dressed, middle-aged secretary for the second time in as many days and announced, "Alex Shepherd to see Mr. Turner."

He didn't miss how her green eyes flickered to a clock hanging on the wall above her desk before she gave him a nod of approval. "Mr. Turner is on a phone call and will be a few more minutes. Please help your-self to a bottle of water and have a seat."

She gestured to a small fridge near the door he'd walked through moments before. It was filled with three-ounce bottles displaying the Paradox logo on the labels.

"Thank you." After grabbing a bottle of water to relieve his parched throat, he sat and glanced around the reception area. In addition to the glass door he'd entered through, three wooden doors leading into other rooms were closed. The furniture was upscale, as expected for an elegant hotel. One wall was covered with stunning black-and-white images of the various hotels and other properties owned by Scout Turner's ever-growing empire. The guy was a fantastic businessman, having reached multi-millionaire status in the hospitality industry before the age of thirty. Forbes, Fortune, Newsweek, and the New York Times were just a few publications featuring in-depth articles about him recently. His business savviness, coupled with his good looks, employees' loyalty, and significant contributions to several charities, had made him a popular public figure.

At three o'clock on the nose, the secretary's phone rang, and she answered the call. "Yes, Mr. Turner, he's here . . . certainly." After hanging up, she pointed to the closed door on her left. "Go on in."

Taking a cleansing breath, Alex pulled himself together, got to his feet, and tossed the now-empty water bottle into a small recycling bin beside the fridge. Out of courtesy, he knocked before pushing the door open. Turner rose from his leather chair behind a large cherrywood desk and held out his hand. "Ready to try this again?"

Alex shook the man's strong hand, trying to ignore how good it felt against his own. "Yes, sir. I apologize again for yesterday. It was completely unprofessional."

"Yet understandable. Have a seat."

The men sat on either side of the desk. Like the rest of the hotel and reception area, the office was decorated in rich tones, fine furnishings, and attractive but unobtrusive artwork. Alex could see his résumé and employment application directly in front of Turner, who relaxed back in his chair and pinned him with an inquisitive stare. "So, tell me something about Alexander Shepherd that I won't find in your résumé or on social media. And, yes, security does check that for me."

Alex had seen too many people crash and burn their careers because of the crap they posted on Facebook, Twitter, or Instagram. Mostly, he avoided the sites except to stay in contact with some friends and family members scattered around the country.

"You mean besides everything I unloaded on you yesterday before I knew who you were?"

Turner's chuckle was deep and sexy and sent a shiver down Alex's spine. "Yes, although that did give me quite a bit of insight about you. Tell me what I don't know already."

Alex wasn't sure what the man wanted him to say. Again, it'd been a long time since he interviewed for a job. "Okay, well, I'm a bit OCD about certain things, which, I'm sure you know, in the hospitality business, isn't a bad thing. I enjoy traveling for both work and pleasure. And aside from when my mother had her stroke and when I had an appendectomy three years ago, I never took any unplanned time off from my job with the Four Seasons. I loved working there, but as I said yesterday, I felt I had to be closer to my family in case they needed me."

Nodding, Turner appeared to mull over that answer for a few moments. Alex hoped his response had been appropriate enough.

Turner picked up a pen and twirled it between his fingers. "You do understand, if you're offered the position, you'll be working long hours for me—fifty to sixty per week. It's Monday through Friday, eight to five, but you'll also be expected to attend late-hour meetings and the occasional weekend event. Those will almost always be scheduled in advance by at least a few days."

"Yes, I understand." The job description posted on an employment site had listed all of that.

"Breakfast and lunch meetings happen frequently as well. But, as you'll probably hear from my employees, I'm not a heartless man. If something happens within your family that needs your attention, I expect you to let me know, and I'll make sure you have the time you need."

"I appreciate that, Mr. Turner."

For the next fifteen minutes, Turner asked questions, and Alex answered them to the best of his ability. While his mind stayed focused on the interview, he still found himself studying the other man. Turner's dark-brown hair went well with his hazel eyes, which were more green than brown—probably because of his emerald-colored tie. He was about an inch or two shorter than Alex's six-foot-two and obviously had a fine physique under his custom-made, dark gray suit. All the images Alex had seen of Turner for the last ten years or so were with him sporting a beard and mustache. It was a sexy look on the man, but so was this clean-shaven one. Alex couldn't decide which he liked better.

As Turner wrapped up the interview, Alex presumed he'd get a phone call in a few days about whether or not he got the job. Undoubtedly, there were dozens of interested applicants vying for the position. When Turner stood and held out his hand, which Alex shook, the last thing he expected was for the man to say, "Welcome to Turner Continental, Alex. Before you leave today, go over to personnel and fill out all the payroll and insurance paperwork. They'll give you an employee packet with all the information you need about the company and assign you a parking space. After that, stop by security to have your picture taken for your employee ID. They'll also fingerprint you for the electronic scanners on some restricted doors and give you a set of keys. Are you available to start tomorrow?"

"Uh . . . um, yes. Yes, sir. I'm sorry. You caught me off guard. Yes, I can start tomorrow."

"Good. Report here first thing in the morning at eight o'clock sharp, and we'll go over what I expect from you as my personal assistant. I purposely have a light schedule this week, but come Monday, be ready to hit the ground running. Are you old school and use a day planner or will a tablet work?"

Another question that caused him to shift gears and make a sharp turn in a different direction. That time, he recovered faster from the verbal whiplash. "A tablet is preferable."

"I'll have one waiting for you in the morning. Delilah will give you directions to personnel on your way out."

Assuming he was dismissed, Alex turned to go but stopped when he remembered his manners. He still reeled from the abrupt job offer. When Turner raised an eyebrow at him, Alex smiled. "Thank you for hiring me, sir. I look forward to working for you and will do my best to get up to speed as soon as possible."

"Good to hear. Oh, by the way, did you bring the dog's vet bill?"

"Um, no, sir, it wasn't ready yet."

Turner nodded as he retook his seat. "That's fine. When you get it, give it to Delilah, and she'll make sure it gets paid."

"I will, Mr. Turner."

"It's Scout, Alex. Mr. Turner or sir are only suited for formal settings."

"Okay, Scout it is. Thanks again."

Alex left the office, controlling the urge to throw a few fist pumps into the air. There would be plenty of time to celebrate later.

After he finished with personnel and security a little

over an hour later, it was dinnertime. The hotel's classy restaurant wasn't something he was into while dining alone, so he exited the building and glanced around. Across the street was a pub that looked pretty good, and Alex chuckled at its name—the Cock & Bull. Since San Francisco had a large LBGTQ+ population, the name was undoubtedly a play on words. He wouldn't be surprised to find it catered to the gay community. When the traffic in front of him came to a stop, he waited for the crossing signal to turn green and joined a small crowd of people making their way to the other side of the street.

Three men entered the pub ahead of him, and the last one held the door open for him, giving him a flirtatious smile as he did so. He was cute but at least ten years Alex's junior. At thirty-four, Alex no longer wanted to date guys who preferred to spend most of their time at clubs and parties.

When the threesome stopped at the hostess stand, Alex stepped around them and found a seat at the bar. He didn't mind eating alone but hated sitting at a table by himself. At the bar, he could probably find some casual conversation or watch sports games or the news on one of the many large TVs hanging on the walls around the area sectioned off from the main dining room.

After ordering a beer and asking for a menu, he took a moment to hang his suit jacket on the back of the stool, loosen his tie, and undo the top button of his shirt before sitting down. A glance around the place told him it was much bigger than it appeared from the outside. The bar took up one whole wall, from front to back, while counter-height tables and chairs were evenly spaced along a half wall behind Alex. On the other side of that, tables and booths surrounded a dance floor in the main dining room. A small stage, which he assumed was for musical entertainment, was at the far end of the room. At the back of the bar was the entrance to the kitchen and a hallway where the restrooms were located. Over by the hostess stand was a set of stairs leading to a second level. An expansive balcony along the entire perimeter held more dining tables and allowed the patrons to observe what was happening below.

The bar and tables were half-filled, but it was still early, and every few minutes, more people flowed in through the front door. It looked like the place did a decent business. If the food was good, Alex might visit often after work.

Before his mind could fully shift back to his new boss, his *hot* new boss, the bartender placed a pint of Guinness and a menu in front of him and asked, "Do I know you? You look really familiar."

Alex eyed the man for a moment—dark hair, brown eyes, broad shoulders, about six-three, and around Alex's age. He thought the other guy was familiar-looking too. Suddenly, a name popped into his head. "Gino Demara?"

A smile spread across the bartender's face, and recognition flashed in his eyes. He reached across the bar for a handshake. "Yeah! Holy crap! Alex Shepherd— that *is* you. I think the last time I saw you was our five-year reunion. How've ya been? *Where've* ya been?"

Gino and Alex attended high school together and were in several classes with each other. While they hadn't been close—their graduating class had over 300 students—they'd still been friends and hung out with many of the same people. "I'm doing great, and I just moved back here from New York. My mom had a stroke, so I came back to help out."

"Aw, that sucks, man. She doing okay, though?"

"Yeah, she is. It just made me realize how much distance there is between New York and here. What are you up to these days?"

Gino shrugged. "Little of this, little of that. For now, I'm working for my cousin, Rico, who owns the place. He's a couple of years older than us, so I'm not sure if you remember him."

He shook his head. The name sounded familiar, but he couldn't conjure up an image of the man. "Not really, no."

"He'll be in later—I'll introduce you. So, where are you working now?"

"Actually, I got hired to work for Scout Turner across the street. Just came from the interview."

Gino's eyes widened. "Seriously? That's awesome. Scout's a great guy and really takes care of his employees. He's good friends with Rico. In fact, he's a silent partner in this place."

Alex filed that surprising tidbit of information away in his mind. It appeared Turner was involved in more business ventures than Alex had uncovered. Although, with his new position, he would learn a lot more about the man.

"Hey, Gino, I need two Heinekens, a chardonnay, and a dirty martini up," a female server at the end of the bar called out to him.

He waved his acknowledgment but turned back to Alex. "Can you stick around after you eat? I get off in about an hour. We'll have a few beers and catch up."

"Sounds good."

As Gino strode toward the end of the bar, Alex picked up the menu. It was amazing how much had changed since yesterday afternoon. A second chance at the interview. A new dream job. Reconnecting with old friends. San Francisco was finally starting to feel like home again. Now, if he could just find someone to adopt that damn adorable dog.

Three

Thankfully, as promised, Thursday and Friday were relatively slow in the Paradox's main office, so Alex was able to ease into the new position while taking lots of notes. He followed Scout around the hotel as his boss introduced him to the various department heads who ran the place as smoothly as possible. Knowing he wouldn't remember everyone's names right off the bat, Alex entered them into an open document on the tablet he'd been given, along with their title and a brief description of their physical appearance to help him recall who they were later on.

Once the weekend rolled around, Scout gave Alex both days off. He mentioned he had family visiting and would only take emergency calls, which were filtered through Delilah until Alex was better acclimated.

Alex took advantage of the free weekend and found a good home for the rescued dog. Now dubbed Sasha, the black-and-white terrier mix was adopted by his sister's friends—a married couple with ten-year-old twins. Scout had not only paid the vet bill but told Alex to give the family a $100 gift card to a local pet store so they could get whatever their new pup needed. Apparently, Scout had a soft spot for animals despite not having any pets of his own.

On Monday, they hit the ground running, as Scout had warned him. Since Alex arrived shortly before 8:00 a.m., there'd been numerous meetings. Some were in person, while others were virtual through Zoom on a large-screen TV in his office as Alex and Scout sat side-by-side at a conference table with a webcam pointed at them.

As Scout wrapped up the last morning meeting with his new Seattle hotel's on-site staff, he was assured the construction crew was on schedule, and everything was ready to move to the next stage. Paradox-North would be open for business within six months if all went as planned.

Alex jotted down a few more details from the meeting using a pen and pad to have the information at his fingertips if Scout needed it. Later, he'd enter them into the tablet when he got a free moment. While it was double work, he didn't want to rely on something that could freeze or reboot itself in the middle of his task, which would result in losing every-thing. That happened once or twice during his tenure at the Four Seasons, so lesson learned. He also backed everything up on the company's own cloud for safe-keeping.

Ending the Zoom meeting, Scout turned to Alex. "That's it until one-thirty, right?"

Alex picked up the tablet and hit the icon for the schedule that only he and Delilah had access to. Locating the information, he read it off. "Actually, your next meeting is at two o'clock with Will Delaney from TKR. Delilah made a note that he called and asked to push it back a half hour. After that, you have to be in Conference Room C to meet with representatives from EnerGen at three. And your four-thirty with Hannah Townsend from Building a Better Tomorrow has been postponed until next week."

"I expected that—saw on the news this morning her father-in-law passed away. He was a state representative for two terms. BBT is Hannah's charity to build housing for homeless veterans. Find out when and where the services are. Tell Delilah to send flowers and make a donation in Richard Townsend's name to BBT. I'll need to attend one of the wakes. If there are two days of them, with afternoon and evening times, mark me down for the second afternoon. Otherwise, make it either evening." As Alex jotted everything in a note to give to the secretary, Scout got to his feet, stepped behind his desk, and retrieved his cell phone and keys. "So, since we have a little extra time before the next meeting, let's head upstairs, grab some lunch, and go over the schedule for the rest of the week."

"Uh, sure." Alex wracked his brain, trying to remember what was above the fourth floor where they could eat. He thought all those floors were guest rooms and condos, but maybe he was mistaken. While he'd eaten lunch with his boss twice now, once was during a meeting in one of the conference rooms, and the other was at Sapphire's.

He followed Scout out of the office, giving Delilah, who was on the phone, a wave as he passed. After he looked up the funeral information, he'd get it to her, along with Scout's request. Instead of taking the nearest elevator, as they'd done during his first two days at work, Scout led Alex to another one at the far end of the hallway and hit the up button.

Scout smiled when he noticed Alex's confused expression. "This is the one for the condo owners only. Hotel guests don't have access to it at all. I can take either the hotel or condo elevator up to my penthouse with a key, but I use this one as much as possible."

Okay, so it sounded like they would eat lunch in his apartment. Alex hadn't been up there yet and was curious to see where Scout lived. When he hung out with Gino the other night for a few beers, Alex learned a little more about his new boss that he hadn't been aware of. The important thing was that Scout's former PA was fired after he developed an unhealthy obsession with him, stalking Scout and messing with his personal life. Gino didn't know all the details but knew enough to paint a broad picture.

While Scout was openly gay, he didn't mix business with pleasure.

Now that he knew about his predecessor, Alex made sure he didn't show any outward attraction to Scout, which was honestly difficult to do. Alex always strived for absolute professionalism during his career at the Four Seasons, but then again, he never lusted over someone he worked with before. Scout Turner was sexy as hell, becoming more so each day. But if Alex wanted to keep his job—and he did—he'd have to ignore all the dirty, porn-worthy images involving Scout being naked that popped into his mind.

Once the elevator arrived, they stepped in, and Scout flashed a key fob over a sensor, then hit the button for the penthouse level. Alex's stomach dropped as the car sped upward. They reached the top floor in under a minute, and the doors opened. Exiting into a large, square vestibule with only two access doors, Scout stepped over to the one on the right and flashed his key fob over another sensor. A light on it turned green, and the door clicked open. As he led the way into his penthouse, Scout pointed to the other door across the way. "By the way, Magnus Keller lives there. Despite his bad-boy reputation, he's a really nice guy and a good friend of mine. Don't get all starry-eyed and tongue-tied around him, and you'll get along with him just fine. Kick your shoes off."

Holy shit. Not only was Scout friends with Hollywood's latest hottest actor, but he lived across the hall from him. It wasn't like Alex hadn't interacted with the numerous celebrities who stayed at the Four Seasons in New York, but damn, Magnus Keller was freaking smokin'. Alex had seen every movie he made so far.

After following Scout's order to remove his shoes in the foyer, Alex eyed his surroundings as he followed Scout into a state-of-the-art kitchen. First, the place was huge. Second, it was a chef's dream. The dark cabinets, black granite countertops, stainless steel appliances, and stone tiling perfectly complemented each other. A half wall allowed anyone in the kitchen to see the rest of the open floor plan of the living room, with several seating sections designed for comfort and a formal dining area. White carpeting explained why he had to take his shoes off.

The great room had tall windows that ran the length of it, showcasing a view of the Golden Gate Bridge and the bay. The furniture appeared classic yet cozy. A white couch with dark green accent cushions, two brown leather recliners, and cherrywood coffee and end tables were arranged in front of a massive stone gas fireplace. Across from the windows, to the left of the entrance to the foyer, was a small, counter-height table and chairs, with a chess game in progress. On the wall behind it were floor-to-ceiling bookcases filled with novels, many with leather covers, some photos, and tchotchkes. In the corner opposite the fireplace, in front of the windows, was a baby grand piano, and Alex wondered if Scout knew how to play it.

Off the great room, on either side, were hallways that presumably led to the bedrooms and maybe an office or something.

"Is grilled cheese okay?" Scout asked, drawing Alex's attention again. He'd shed his suit jacket and hung it on the back of a stool at the island. His head was buried in the open fridge as he took out the fixings for lunch, and Alex tried not to stare at the guy's fine ass.

"Um, yeah, that sounds good. Thanks."

He glanced over his shoulder and smirked at Alex. "You sound hesitant about my cooking abilities. I may not be a five-star chef, but I do well enough not to poison myself or anyone else."

Alex couldn't help the laugh that escaped him. "That's . . . uh, that's good to know. No poison. Good. Can I help with anything?"

Selecting a frying pan from the hanging rack over the room's island, Scout pointed to two separate cabinets and a drawer. "Plates are in there, glasses there, and silverware. You can set the table while I'm cooking." He gestured toward a round table for two in a nook in the corner of the room. "There's also a container of summer slaw, pickles, and a pitcher of sweet tea in the fridge—you can put them out too. If you prefer soda, there's some in the pantry over there. Feel free to take your jacket off."

For the next few minutes, they worked in an easy silence. Alex removed his jacket and hung it on the back of a second stool, then found everything where he was told it would be. There were already fabric placemats and napkins on the table. Once he was done with his assignments, Alex watched Scout fry their sandwiches. The man had rolled up his sleeves and donned a black apron and still looked sexy as hell.

Alex had difficulty keeping his gaze off Scout, so he forced himself to focus on the food instead. "That looks better than any grilled cheese I've ever had."

"White cheddar, brie, Monterey Jack, and gruyere on sourdough bread. Mayo and butter on the outside and fried to perfection. Gourmet comfort food at its best."

"Smells like it."

Scout grinned at the compliment. "So, do you like the job so far, compared to your old one?"

Alex was glad he didn't have to lie. "I like it a lot. You have a different way of doing a few things, but nothing I can't adjust to. It's a beautiful hotel, and your employees and guests seem to love it. Do you mind if I ask how you got into the business?"

"Not at all, but let me take care of this first." He turned off the stove, carried the frying pan to the table, and then used a spatula to place a sandwich on each plate. "Sit."

Alex obeyed the command as Scout dumped the pan and utensil into the sink and turned the water on briefly before joining him at the table. After taking a pickle spear and a scoop of the slaw and adding them to his plate, Alex cut his sandwich in half and picked one up. He was aware that the other man watched him take the first bite. A burst of cheesy deliciousness hit his taste buds, and he couldn't help but moan in delight. Scout just laughed and then took a bite of his own sandwich.

Alex chewed and swallowed, nodding the entire time. Before he spoke, he wiped his mouth with a napkin. "Holy cow, this has to be the most incredible grilled cheese sandwich I've ever had."

"Ass-kissing the boss isn't necessary, Alex."

"Trust me, that wasn't an attempt to ass-kiss. This is really, *really* good." He took another bite and noticed a pleased expression on Scout's face. The man seemed relieved that his assistant liked the meal he cooked for them. Alex wondered what it would be like to sit there, having breakfast with Scout after a night of raunchy sex.

Nope, don't think that. He's off-limits, Shepherd—if you want to keep your job, that is!

"So, you asked how I got into the hotel business," Scout said after sipping his soda.

"Mm-hmm." That was all he could say with a mouthful of food.

"My dad's got a successful real estate investment company—condos, townhouses, private neighborhoods, stuff like that. Growing up, I got to do a lot of traveling all over the US and Canada for Dad's business, then to other countries for vacations. My parents aim to visit as many of the world's greatest cities and places as possible before they die. My two younger sisters and I were on our third passports by the time we hit our twenties."

"Wow. And I've never been out of the States except for Canada and a few trips to the Caribbean."

"Yeah, well, since we spent so much time traveling, I began using my own system to rate hotels and restaurants. At first, it was just for fun. I kept track of all the little details that made a place unique—things that weren't common everywhere we went. Then, as I grew older, I realized what I could do with all that information.

"With my dad as a backer, I bought my first place in Santa Ana when I was twenty-six. Long story short, I flipped it for a nice profit two years later. By then, I was hooked. The next one I invested in, I kept. That was the beginning of Turner Continental. Ten years later, here I am, getting ready to open my seventh hotel, with a few other ventures under my belt too."

Alex swallowed the last bite of his sandwich, almost disappointed it was all gone. "That's fantastic. You found something you loved to do and created a successful business from it."

"So, what about you? How'd you get into the hotel industry?"

"Honestly, it wasn't my original choice of majors.

When I first got to NYU, I wanted to get a business admin degree. We lived in New York until I was fourteen, and I missed it enough to want to go back there for school. To help my folks with the tuition and other expenses, I got a job at the Roxy in Tribeca as a bellman. Made good money in tips and started learning more about the business. I switched majors after two years but kept biz admin as my minor. Graduated and ended up at the Four Seasons."

"Then you ended up here." He lifted his glass of soda and held it up in the air. Alex clinked his glass against Scout's as the man continued. "Well then, here's to new beginnings. Glad to have you on my staff."

For some unknown, messed-up reason, Alex's brain altered that last sentence, and he almost choked—*Glad to have you on my shaft.*

Four

Six weeks later . . .

It wasn't even five in the morning yet, and Scout already pounded away on the treadmill in his home gym, sweat pouring off him as he tried to expel a few demons from his brain. Like almost every day for the past month and a half, he'd woken up hard as stone with his PA's name on his lips. Never had he fantasized about one man, who he'd never even kissed, for this long before, and it got worse as time went by.

Last night, Scout stayed up late, playing the piano, something he did often when indecision plagued him. He had an eclectic mix of favorite composers and songwriters whose songs he could play by ear. A little Elton John, Billy Joel, or Carole King tended to soothe him whenever he was in a funk, while Beethoven, Mozart, and Jerry Lee Lewis were his composers of choice for his personal form of anger management. Yanni, Norah Jones, and John Tesh were his go-to artists when he was in a romantic mood. Maybe he'd try a little bit of Ludwig, Wolfgang, and Jerry Lee tonight since Elton, Billy, and Carole hadn't worked.

He'd tried several things, short of dragging the man into his bed and fucking the daylights out of him, to keep thoughts of Alex where they belonged—in the business-only section of his mind. So far, nothing had been successful. The horny toad on his shoulder urged him to give in to his lust. But the workhorse on the other side kept telling him not to rock the boat and ruin a good thing.

Alex was an excellent PA—the best Scout had ever hired—and it had nothing to do with the man's good looks or how much Scout was drawn to him. It hadn't taken Alex long to get into the swing of things—he picked up on the routine around there quickly and got along well with the other Paradox employees. If Scout told him to do something, his assistant got it done with minimal effort or explanation. He was always on top of things, sometimes even ahead of Scout's orders. A few times, Scout kiddingly called Alex "Radar" after the character in *M*A*S*H*, who always knew what would happen before it actually did.

It amazed Scout how comfortable he was around Alex—if one didn't count his perpetual hard-on. Many afternoons, they enjoyed lunch in Scout's penthouse, discussing everything under the sun. Hell, he'd rarely brought Erik up there for any reason, but with Alex, it felt right. They had much in common and interesting debates on things they disagreed on. It'd gotten to the point that Scout hated to see their lunch breaks end and work start up again.

He noticed he was in a sour mood in the mornings lately before Alex showed up and brightened his world. And at the end of the workday, more than once, he invited Alex to dinner at Sapphire's or the Cock & Bull —anything so not to say goodnight to the man. However, he drew the line at asking Alex to have dinner at his place. With lunch, they needed to go back to work afterward, so Scout had a reason not to start anything, but with no plans after dinner, he'd be tempted to seduce his PA. Nope. He wasn't going there because it was a recipe for disaster. He just had to keep telling himself that, and maybe, someday, it would sink in.

Ever since he found out for certain that Alex was gay, or at least bisexual, he fantasized, both day and night, about having the man naked and at his mercy. During one of the happy hours they attended at the pub, he overheard Alex talking to Gino about a guy he'd dated in New York for about eighteen months. They broke up about two months before Mrs. Shepherd had her stroke, and it was the nail in the coffin, so to speak, that helped him decide to move back to the West Coast. Apparently, it hadn't been a healthy relationship for Alex—the ex-boyfriend was extremely needy—and he was glad it was over.

The treadmill beeped rapidly, indicating Scout had hit his programmed four-mile mark. He stabbed a button that slowed the belt to a leisurely walk so he could cool down. A minute later, he turned the machine off and grabbed a nearby towel to wipe the sweat off his face before chugging a bottle of water. The cool liquid quenched his thirst but did nothing to dispel the heat he felt as Alex's face popped into his mind—again—which caused his cock to harden painfully.

"Argh. Fuck this!" He stormed out of the room and headed for the shower. He was going to have to jack off in there if he had any hope of hiding his lust from Alex when the guy showed up for work in three hours.

He stripped off his clothes as soon as he entered his bedroom on his way to the en suite bath, tossing them in a hamper. While the hotel maids cleaned his place twice weekly, he had a small laundry nook on the other side of the room's massive walk-in closet. He didn't like the notion of someone handling his clothing, especially his underwear, so he did it himself. While the building was still in its planning and construction phases, he sat down with the architect and an interior designer to give input on every minute detail he wanted included. Not once, since he moved in, had he wished he'd asked for something forgotten or miscalculated.

While letting the water in the shower warm up,

Scout checked his appearance in the vanity mirror above the dual sinks. A month after losing the bet that forced him to shave off his beard and mustache, he let them grow back in, but not as heavy as before. Alex had casually mentioned one day that Scout looked really good with the scruffy-but-not-*too*-scruffy look, so now, he kept his facial hair trimmed short. If he were honest, he preferred the updated look too.

Within minutes, he was in his oversized shower stall with hot water pelting him from three sides and above. Scout grabbed a bottle of lube he kept handy and squirted some into his palm. Placing his other hand against the stone-tiled wall, he grasped his stiff cock. He started slowly, stroking himself from tip to root and back again. His eyes fluttered shut as images of Alex on his knees in front of him filtered into his mind. He envisioned the man's mouth opening and taking his full length inside. A groan rumbled from his chest past his lips. "Suck me, Alex. God damn it, suck me hard!"

He tightened his grip and quickened the pace. The scene in his mind switched to the other man kneeling on his bed, facedown in the comforter, ass in the air. As much as he wanted to savor the fantasy, Scout couldn't take the anticipation and fast-forwarded until he was fucking Alex's puckered hole. The guy begged him to go faster and harder, and Scout was more than happy to oblige.

Without warning, his orgasm hit him like a ton of

bricks. Pure pleasure raced through him, engulfing him. His mind spun out of control, briefly going offline as he cried out and shot cum into his hand. It over-flowed and fell, mixing with the water going down the drain.

Pivoting, he let the wall hold him up as his legs shook from the monumental orgasm he just experienced. As he got his breathing under control, he looked down at the shower's tiled floor, visualizing Alex kneeling there with a satisfied grin on his handsome face. Scout shook his head and whispered to the figment of his imagination, "Alex, Alex, Alex, what the hell am I going to do about you?"

The Cock & Bull was packed, filled with locals and tourists alike, celebrating the end of the work week. As usual, as five o'clock rolled around, he hadn't wanted to say goodbye to Alex—especially since he had nothing planned that required his assistance over the weekend. Unable to resist, Scout invited Alex to happy hour and dinner. Since many of his friends were there, as usual on Fridays, he was able to divert his attention so he didn't seem overly focused on his PA. He didn't want to raise the man's suspicions that more than a business relationship was forming between them.

They managed to grab two seats at the bar and were on their second round of drinks—Guinness for Alex and Grey Goose and club soda with a twist of lime for Scout. Tending the bar were the owner, Rico Demara, his cousin, Gino, and Austin Haynes, one of the regular Friday night servers. The other bartender had called in sick again, and Rico told him not to bother coming back.

Scout's old friend did a great job running the place. It had already received several positive write-ups in various newspapers and online sites. Within two weeks of opening, the Cock & Bull became the newest hotspot in San Francisco.

Weaving his way through the crowd, Scout returned from the bathroom and clenched his jaw when he saw yet another guy hitting on Alex. The ridiculously attractive man drew them in like flies to honey, but as far as Scout could tell, not a single guy in the past few weeks had gotten Alex's phone number. Of course, that hadn't stopped some of them from giving him theirs, on a business card or handwritten note, if he was ever in the mood to hook up.

Forcing himself not to glare at the asshole blatantly flirting with Alex, Scout, again, took his seat next to his PA, whose back was currently to him. Even though Scout hadn't made a sound or touched him, Alex glanced over his shoulder as if he sensed his return.

"Hey, I was waiting for you to get back." He held up his cell phone and stood. "My dad called, but it was too loud to take the call, and I didn't want to leave our seats unattended. I'll be right back."

Scout's gaze shifted to the man on the other side of Alex, who seemed disappointed he lost his seduction target's attention. A rush of satisfaction shot through Scout.

Yup, another one bites the dust. Thank God.

"Yeah, sure. Take your time. Hope everything is okay."

As Alex headed for the front door, Scout picked up his vodka and soda and took a sip. Behind the bar, Rico walked over and slid a plate of potato skins in front of him. The dish was one of Scout's favorite appetizers the chef had on the menu. They weren't your typical potato skins with bacon bits, cheddar cheese, and scallions. Nope. All that was replaced by pureed artichokes with goat cheese, garlic, fresh herbs, and olive oil. They were so freaking delicious, and he'd eat them every day of the week if it weren't for the excessive carbs and calories.

Scout raised an eyebrow at Rico, who gestured toward the bar's front door. "Your boy ordered them."

While he doubted his friend meant anything by "Your boy" other than a way of referring to Alex as his PA, Scout still liked how the phrase made him feel. He wanted Alex to be his but didn't want to screw up the status quo.

"And I can practically see those wheels spinning in your mind," Rico said with a smirk. He leaned on his forearms, closing the distance between them so he could lower his voice. His dark-brown hair was fashioned in a fade style, a little longer than a crewcut on top, diminishing to fully shaved on the sides. With his hazel eyes, a shadow of stubble over his firm jawline, a deep baritone voice, and a lean, solid body, the man garnered much interest from both men and women. Unfortunately for the women, Rico didn't swing their way. "I take it he doesn't know his boss wants to jump his bones."

His eyes widened. "What the hell are you talking about?"

"Seriously, Scout? This is me that you're trying to bullshit. You never got a jealous look on your face whenever some guy hit on Erik, no matter how hard he tried to push your buttons. Hell, I don't think I've ever seen you this jealous over anyone you've dated, either."

Scout ran a hand down his face, his five-o'clock shadow rasping against his palm. "Shit. Is it that fucking obvious?"

"Only to someone who's known you as long as I have."

The two had met in junior high and hit it off almost immediately. However, there was never any sexual attraction between them. Even though they were both gay, they developed more of a sibling relationship than anything else. While Rico was very handsome now, they were gawky teenagers back then, still unsure of their individual sexual orientation. By the time they outgrew their awkward stages and realized they were both into guys, neither wanted to risk their close friendship by experimenting. And that's all it would've been—an experiment—so they never crossed that line with each other.

"So, the way I see it, there are three possibilities here. One, you keep things on a professional level and go to sleep sexually frustrated every night and wake up the same way in the morning. Two, you have a brief fling, and in the aftermath, there's too much uncomfortable tension between you two, so you either fire him or he quits."

"Aren't *you* just an optimistic unicorn jumping over a rainbow tonight?"

Rico snorted. "I've been shitting glitter all day, buddy. And you didn't let me get to the third option before you got on your high horse."

"Do tell."

"Three, you discover he's the guy you've waited for all your life. The one you fall in love with and live happily ever after with."

Scout gaped at him. "You're not helping, dude. Even if I thought number three was possible, do I want to risk number two being the winner or, technically, the loser in this mess?"

"If you really care for him, isn't having him yours, in every way possible, for the rest of your life worth that risk?"

And that was the question plaguing Scout for the next two hours as he and Alex enjoyed dinner and each other's company.

Five

Feeling buzzed, embarrassed, and nervous as all hell, Alex followed Scout through the Paradox lobby toward the elevators. While having a great time at the Cock & Bull, he didn't realize how much he had to drink until he started to sway on his feet, and Scout grabbed his arm to steady him.

Great, just great.

He'd done the one thing he swore he would never do—have too much to drink in the presence of his boss and a few coworkers who'd joined them during the evening. After the swaying, Scout demanded Alex's car keys and, instead of calling an Uber or cab for him, quietly told him he could crash in the penthouse. Alex didn't have to work in the morning, and since he'd parked in the private lot, there was a good chance he could sneak out after getting a few hours of sleep without doing a walk of shame. At least, he could save face in that respect. Not that it would be an actual walk of shame since he wouldn't be sleeping with Scout. Instead, he would spend a few hours in one of the man's spare bedrooms. Either way, it would be awkward leaving in the morning.

Scout hadn't appeared mad or upset with him—in fact, he seemed quite amused at the turn of events. So, why was Alex nervous? Because he was afraid that he'd do something stupid in his inebriated state—like confessing his non-professional feelings for his boss.

They ended up alone in the elevator, and Scout flashed his fob over the sensor before hitting the button for the penthouse level. Alex's stomach dropped as it always did when the car lifted, carrying them up to the forty-first floor. His gaze was on his feet, but through his eyelashes, he watched as Scout leaned against the wall and crossed his arms and ankles. Alex's heart raced as he fought the urge to drag his gaze up the other man's body in an obvious ogling.

He had no idea how many floors they passed or how many they still had to go before Scout cleared his throat. The soft sound caused Alex to lift his head. His gaze slammed into Scout's, and he could swear he saw heat and interest in it. But then again, he was one drink shy of being totally drunk, so he could be mistaken.

Unless his mind had played tricks on him, like he thought it was doing now, Alex could swear his boss drank just as much as he had, but the man didn't appear wasted. In fact, he looked dead sober.

"Can I ask you something?"

Alex shivered at the rumbling voice, which seemed to be an octave lower than usual. "Um, yeah, sure."

A ding sounded, and the elevator stopped. As the doors slid open, Scout said, "Hold on . . . let's take this inside."

Alex followed him to the door and then into the penthouse. But instead of continuing past the foyer, Scout spun around and stepped forward, forcing Alex to reverse his direction until his back hit the door. The other man closed the distance between them until it was mere inches. Alex swallowed a sudden lump in his throat. He felt the heat of Scout's body and smelled the aroma of his woodsy cologne.

They just stood there for a minute or two, staring at each other. Alex's heart rate spiked even higher than it was in the elevator. His breathing also increased. Scout's gaze roamed Alex's face, lingering for long moments on his mouth. They were in each other's personal space, and neither backed down. Not that Alex had an escape route. A solid door was behind him, with a very enticing male in front of him. That knowledge made his blood heat up and rush south to his cock.

Oh, shit. He had a hard-on for his boss, *in front of* his boss!

"Don't you want to know what my question was?"

Huh? Alex's somewhat mushy brain scrambled to

make sense of the murmured question about a question. "Um . . ."

"In the elevator, I wanted to ask you something." God, the man's deep, raspy voice was sexier than ever tonight. When had it changed, and what had made the difference?

He thought back to the elevator ride. Right before they reached the top floor, Scout said something about a question. "Um, yeah, right. What—" He gulped, trying to force down the lump still in his throat. "What did you want to know?"

A sensual smile appeared on Scout's face. "If I said I wanted to kiss you, would you let me?"

Oh.

My.

God.

Okay, this was not happening. He was drunk and passed out somewhere, dreaming it up. That had to be it. So, if it was a dream, he may as well play out the fantasy, right? Or was he imagining it was a dream? Did that even make sense?

Pain shot through his abdomen, and he looked down to see Scout had pinched him. Not hard enough to bruise, but it definitely got his attention. "Eyes up, Alex. You're not dreaming or imagining things. I asked you a question and expect an answer."

Scout knew he stepped over the line and could never undo his actions, but between his intense desire for this man and Rico's pep talk, he was helpless to stop himself. He knew Alex wasn't feeling much pain at the moment, but he wasn't too drunk. As for Scout, he was pretty damn sober. Rico, Gino, Austin, and the other bartenders at the Cock & Bull and the Paradox knew to put less and less vodka in his drinks as the night wore on. By the fourth round, the only things in his glass were club soda and ice with a lime twist. It was how he still appeared to drink socially while staying in an alert frame of mind, which became handy during many of his after-hours business meetings over the years.

While he could've waited until they were both sober, he wanted to take advantage of Alex's defenses being down. He wouldn't have sex with the man tonight—as much as his cock wanted to—but he wanted to see if they could start taking a few steps in that direction. It wasn't a fling he wanted—not with Alex.

For the first time in . . . well, for the first time ever, he saw himself in a long-term relationship with one man. Rico was right—if Scout didn't take a chance, he'd never know. Something extraordinary might come from this—he just had to take things slowly. The last thing he wanted Alex to think was that he did this often because he didn't. Scout had never dated an employee or a business associate. But seeing Alex every day and being unable to touch and kiss him was torturous, to say the least.

The heat from Alex's body penetrated two layers of clothing and radiated across Scout's skin. The man's mouth looked delectable, as it always did, and the only thing preventing him from kissing it was Alex still hadn't given him an answer.

Desire filled Alex's eyes, but also a bit of wariness.

Scout reached up and stroked the other man's stubbled cheek. Whatever aftershave Alex put on that morning still lingered, just enough to tantalize Scout's sense of smell. "It's okay. If you say no, we'll forget I ever asked." As if he could. "If you say yes, it'll just be a kiss—nothing more. I've never done this before, Alex—not with someone who worked for me. But there's something about you . . . I just can't . . . I can't resist. I want you and for more than just one night. And that kind of scares me a little." More like a lot. "But don't worry, your job is safe either way. The decision is all yours."

Alex licked his lips, drawing a groan from Scout's throat. His cock grew harder, and he knew it would take all his strength not to go any further than just a kiss—*if* Alex said yes.

"You have three seconds to answer me. If you don't, I'll let you sleep in one of the spare bedrooms, and we'll go back to being employer and employee. Three seconds. One . . . two . . ."

"Yes."

The one word had been spoken so softly that Scout almost didn't hear it. To be sure, he slid his hand to Alex's nape and squeezed gently. "Say it again. I want no misunderstandings between us."

Alex cleared his throat. "I . . . um . . . I said yes."

Scout searched the man's eyes and face for any regret or fear. When he was confident they were both on the same page, he tugged on Alex's neck until only an inch separated their mouths. He didn't want to rush it. There was something amazing about sharing a first kiss. Call him old-fashioned, but he thought it was the sexiest thing in the world—a once-in-a-lifetime experience between two people that could never be duplicated.

His lips brushed against Alex's. Once. Twice. The third time, he didn't break contact. Slowly, he learned the texture and taste of Alex's lips. They were pillowy soft with a firmness underneath, a strength he held back. Scout wanted desperately to unleash the beast within himself, the one dying to strip Alex naked and fuck him until neither of them could walk. But that wouldn't happen tonight. Baby steps. He had to take baby steps because the pending romantic relationship with Alex was too special to screw up before they ever got started.

Scout moved forward, closing the last distance between their bodies, and pinned Alex against the wall, pressing their torsos and pelvises together. Alex was just as hard as Scout, and that knowledge had him wanting to drop to his knees to find out exactly how big and long the man's cock was.

Their hands stroked and squeezed each other's shoulders and upper arms. Scout didn't know about Alex, but he forced himself not to let his hands roam anywhere else, knowing it would lead to stripping the other man naked.

He ran his tongue along Alex's lips, silently asking for entry. When access was granted, he surged inside, licking and savoring. He could taste the Guinness the man enjoyed earlier.

A moan escaped Alex, evoking one in response from Scout. The room grew hotter, or at least it felt that way. Scout needed to stop but kept telling himself to revel in the kiss for a few more seconds.

The slamming of a door had the men jumping apart, breathing heavily. Alex's eyes were wide as they darted around, searching for the source of the noise, but Scout chuckled. "Sorry about that. Sounds like Magnus just got home. If we were further into the apartment, we probably wouldn't have heard it, but since we're against the front door . . ." He shrugged and then cupped Alex's jaw. "Sleep in my bed tonight. No sex. I just want you beside me all night. Please?"

His heart pounded in his chest as he waited for an answer. When a smile spread across Alex's face, Scout knew he had it.

Six

As he stirred, Alex wondered why it was so damn hot in his bedroom. The air conditioning was always set for seventy degrees in his apartment, so he shouldn't be sweating like he was right then. Maybe the power went out during the night.

He tried to kick off the covers, but his heel hit something hard. Before he could figure out what it was, an arm came around his torso, and a soft voice murmured, "Stop kicking me and go back to sleep."

Huh? What the . . .?

Keeping his body stiff, he slowly opened his eyes and let them adjust to the faint morning light filtering in from behind the blinds covering a row of windows. He recognized the room instantly, having been in Scout's bedroom several times before to retrieve things for him.

Oh, shit. What have I done?

His mind scrambled to piece together how he'd ended up in his boss's bed . . . *with* his boss spooning him!

A rush of memories of the night before swirled in his mind like a mini tornado. Cock & Bull. Drinks. Fun. Not allowed to drive home. *You can crash at my place. No worries.* Walking back to the Paradox with Scout. Taking the elevator to the penthouse. A question. Scout had asked him a question.

Oh.

My.

God!

They'd kissed. Hell, they'd made out! In the foyer. Shit! Who initiated it? What else did they do?

Alex took a personal inventory. He was barechested, and his pants were gone, but he was still in his boxer briefs. Okay, that was a good sign, right? If they'd had sex, he probably wouldn't have put them back on. Right?

As hard as he wracked his brain, he couldn't remember what happened after they stopped kissing by the front door.

Shit! How much did I have to drink last night?

He didn't feel that hungover—just a mild headache and a dry mouth—so it shouldn't have been too much.

Panic assailed Alex, and his heart rate sped up. The arm around his body squeezed him. "You're thinking too much." Scout's lips brushed against Alex's bare neck, sending goose bumps skittering across his flesh and blood rushing to his morning wood. "We didn't do anything but kiss. I asked if we could, and you said yes. We didn't have sex, and we're not going to this morning either, as much as I would love to fuck the hell out of you."

He paused, and Alex couldn't think of a thing to say to fill the silence. Being in bed with this man was his fantasy come true. Well, sort of. In his fantasies, they'd done a lot more than just kiss.

Did Scout do this often? With his other PAs or employees? Alex didn't think so. In fact, Scout's words from last night popped into his mind. *I've never done this before, Alex—not with someone who worked for me. But there's something about you . . . I just can't . . . I can't resist. I want you and for more than just one night. And that kind of scares me a little.*

Behind him, Scout let out a heavy sigh. "You're still overthinking this, so let's see what we can do about it. Do you have plans for today?"

It was Saturday, and nothing on Scout's schedule required him to work today. "Um . . ." His voice cracked, and he cleared his throat before trying to speak again. "Uh, no. No plans."

"Good. I want to take you on a bike ride. We'll have lunch and talk. If you want, you can stay here, sleep a while longer, and then shower and borrow some of my clothes. We should be about the same size. Or, you can go home and do whatever you need to do there, and I'll swing by to get you around ten. It's seven now if you were wondering."

"A bike ride? I don't have a bike yet. Been meaning to get a new one." His ten-speed was stolen a few weeks before he left New York City, and he hadn't had a chance to replace it yet.

"Not a bicycle—on my motorcycle. Is it safe to assume you don't own one?"

"Um, yeah. I mean, no, I don't own one."

Scout kissed Alex's back again, sending a shiver down his spine. "Good. I'd rather you ride behind me today. I'm going to go back to sleep for a bit. Are you staying, or should I pick you up at your place?"

Definitely choice number two. Alex had to get out of there so he could have time to think about what already happened and what *might* happen between them before they talked again. "I . . . uh . . . I'm going to run home if that's okay."

"Whatever you want to do is fine with me, babe. Just promise you'll take a ride with me later."

He shouldn't. He really shouldn't. Not if he wanted to keep his job, which is what he'd lose if this . . . whatever this was went south. Unfortunately, "no" was not what came out of his mouth. "I promise."

With a final squeeze, Scout released him and rolled onto his back. When Alex flipped the covers to the side, he noticed a small pillow lying between where his ass and Scout's pelvis had been. The other man was also shirtless. One leg and hip peeked out from under the sheet, revealing he only wore a pair of navy blue boxer shorts.

Alex's gaze shot to Scout's eyes, and he found the other man watching him from under partially-opened lids. A blush stole over Scout's face, along with a sheepish expression. "What can I say? I would've been too tempted without something between us."

Well, at least one of them had been thinking a little clearer than the other at some point last night. Thank God.

As Alex stood and sorted through his and Scout's clothes piled in a heap on the floor, his boss closed his eyes and shifted until he was comfortable. "Before you leave, what's your sub preference? I'll have the bistro pack us a lunch."

"Um . . ." Pulling on his pants, Alex hesitated. For the life of him, he couldn't think of a single thing off the bistro's menu. "Uh . . . anything's fine. Surprise me."

Scout hadn't disappointed him with any of the meals he'd cooked for them over the past month and a half, and after their first lunch, the man asked what foods Alex didn't care for so he could avoid them.

"Sounds good." His eyes remained shut. "See you at ten. Wear jeans, boots, and a leather jacket if you have one."

"Uh . . . okay." Alex checked to make sure he had his wallet, phone, and . . . shit! His keys! "Um . . . Scout? Where are my keys?"

"On the little table in the foyer," he murmured, sleep dragging him under again. "Drive safe."

After one last glance back at the bed and the incredibly sexy man in it, Alex quietly left the room. He needed time to think and stop the whirlwind of questions and "what-ifs" flying through his head. He just hoped he hadn't screwed himself out of a job.

Scout hoped he was doing the right thing. But it was too late to take back his confession and actions, so the only option was to forge ahead.

Under his thighs and ass, his Harley Davidson Fat Boy 114 purred like a contented feline. It was weeks since he last took it out for a ride, something he did whenever he wanted to clear his head. However, it was the first time he'd ever invited someone out on a date on his bike. And, yup, if things went as he planned, he would consider this his and Alex's first date. One of many. The man was special and could very possibly be *the one.*

While he'd been in several relationships over the years that lasted longer than a month, Scout could never see himself in a lifetime commitment with any of those men. He usually made it clear when he first started dating someone that he wasn't looking for anything long-term—just someone to spend time with —and whenever the other men seemed to expect more from him, he ended things. But with Alex . . . God, he could see them growing old together, maybe even having kids. Scout wanted to take the man to all his favorite places worldwide. If they had children, he wanted to raise them as his parents had him—working on their third passport before they reached twenty-one and showing them all the great wonders to explore.

Earlier, after Alex left—he kind of figured the guy would need some alone time to think about everything that happened—Scout hadn't been able to fall back into a deep sleep. His body was willing, but he couldn't shut down his brain. Finally, he gave up and went into his home gym to run a few miles on the treadmill. Then, after showering, he called down to the bistro and asked them to pack a lunch for two that he could put in the Harley's saddlebags. Once that was done, he realized he didn't have Alex's home address. That was easily remedied by accessing the man's personnel file.

Now, as he pulled into the parking lot of a pleasant but plain-looking apartment complex, his nerves seemed to rattle along with the bike. He hoped like hell this worked out between them because he didn't know what he'd do if Alex decided to quit over it.

When he parked in front of building number four, he saw Alex striding toward him, wearing black boots, faded blue jeans, and a San Francisco 49ers' T-shirt. He carried a black leather jacket over one shoulder. It was the first time Scout had seen Alex in casual clothes, and he looked fantastic. The shirt and jeans molded to his trim body and long legs. The man was delicious-looking, and Scout's cock sprung to life. It was obvious Alex had been waiting for him, which pleased Scout more than he expected it to. Damn, he was falling for this man—hard!

Scout killed the engine, then unstrapped the extra helmet from the seat behind him and held it out to Alex as he approached. "Here you go. We're going to ride up 101 for about an hour to this spot I know. It's the perfect place for lunch." The beautiful late April day was ideal for his planned picnic—it wasn't too hot or cold.

"Sounds good." It was clear Alex was nervous, but that wasn't surprising. At least he was there and hadn't ghosted Scout.

He waited as Alex pulled on his jacket and the helmet. Once the man was set, Scout gestured to the seat behind him. "Climb on."

Alex hesitated momentarily, then placed his hand on Scout's shoulder and swung his leg over the seat before settling in. His strong legs straddled Scout's ass and thighs while his hands loosely held onto Scout's hips. And that wouldn't do. Scout gently grabbed Alex's wrists and pulled until the man's arms embraced his waist. When he was sure they'd stay there, he let go and started the engine again.

Within minutes, they were on the highway heading north. Scout loved the feel of Alex's chest against his back and that Alex's arms were still around him. As the

Harley ate up the miles, Alex seemed to relax more and more.

About forty-five minutes into the ride, Scout exited the highway. As he made rights and lefts he memorized years ago, the streets became smaller and less crowded until there were no houses, businesses, or other vehicles to be seen. He easily found the turnoff for the dirt path that would take them to his favorite spot. Trees and brush bracketed them as he slowed the bike to almost a crawl. While he never ran into anyone else whenever he was there, others had to know about the place and drove motorcycles or ATVs on the path because it was never impassable.

When they reached a small clearing, Scout stopped the bike next to a large boulder and turned off the engine. He almost wished they hadn't arrived because Alex let go of him and sat back. Scout leaned forward and allowed the man to dismount first before engaging the kickstand and removing his helmet. Lifting his leg, he got off the bike and stretched his limbs. Without the noise from the Harley, the sounds of nature and wildlife could be heard.

The boulder sat atop a cliff that looked down over a river about forty or fifty feet below. An abundance of trees gave them plenty of shade from the bright sun, which had climbed higher in the sky during their ride. It was his favorite place to come and unwind by himself for a few hours. Sometimes, he brought a book with him, while other times, he just took a walk and explored for a while.

Taking off his leather jacket, he draped it over the bike's seat and told Alex to do the same as he opened the saddlebags and retrieved their lunch. "Come on. We'll eat up here and then take a walk for a bit. I don't know about you, but I didn't have breakfast—just coffee."

"I didn't even have that." He followed as Scout led him around the back side of the boulder to the most accessible spot where they could climb onto it. "It's beautiful up here. How'd you find it?"

Good, the man was engaging in conversation and not just in response to Scout's questions or commands.

"Completely by accident. It is one of those 'Should I go left or right?' types of things. One day, I saw the dirt road and decided to see where it led. I've been back many times since." At the top of the boulder, he gestured to their surroundings. "I love it up here. It's so peaceful that I sometimes lose track of time."

He pivoted to face Alex and elected to put his heart on the line. "This is the first time I've ever brought someone with me. I kind of hoped this could be our first date." When Alex's eyes bugged out, Scout quickly continued. "I know you weren't expecting this, Alex. Neither was I. But I can't help how I feel. I've never been attracted to a man to the point of obsession before, but I can't stop thinking about you. When you walk into the office in the morning, you light up my world. And when you leave for the day, I just want the hours to speed by until I can see you again. I meant what I said—your job isn't at risk whether or not something happens between us. I just know that if I didn't at least try for something more with you, I'd always regret it."

Okay, the guy still gaped at him but hadn't shaken his head or taken off running. That was a good sign, right?

"Listen, all I'm asking for is a chance to see where this goes between us. I can't be the only one feeling this intense attraction. Am I wrong?"

Swallowing hard, Alex shook his head. "No, you're not wrong. But, honestly, I'm a little freaked out. I've never been involved with someone I worked for or with before. But this . . . this thing . . ." He gestured between them. "It's definitely not one-sided. Can we take it slowly, though? I don't want to fuck things up."

When Scout snorted, Alex's eyes narrowed at him. "What?"

A grin spread across Scout's face. "Nothing. That's just the first time you've ever cursed in front of me. I was starting to think it was a religious thing or something. It also tells me you're getting more comfortable with me, and I like that. But I'm okay with taking it slowly. Just know I want to kiss you again, and I plan to do it soon. Now, c'mon, I'm hungry."

Seven

Alex sat on the boulder and found a comfortable position while Scout opened the bags and produced their lunches. The subs were turkey, Gouda cheese, tomato, avocado, and chipotle mayo on whole grain rolls, one of the most popular options on the bistro's menu. Small covered cups of macaroni salad, two bottles of ginger ale, some chips, and a couple of oranges accompanied them. Napkins and forks had also been provided. It was a perfect little picnic. Alex tried remembering the last time he'd been on a picnic but couldn't recall when. Evidently, it hadn't been memorable. However, he was pretty sure he'd remember this one.

Scout was right. It was beautiful there. The sights, sounds, and smells of nature bombarded Alex's senses. The area reminded him of the Catskills in upstate New York. He never went off the beaten path this far north while growing up in San Fransisco and could only imagine what the area would look like in a few months when the leaves started changing to their autumn colors. Alex would love to come back up and see it then.

They were in the shade, under a canopy of Douglas fir, maple, and redwood trees, and there was a nice breeze coming from the west. The air was fresh and crisp. A majestic hawk circled overhead, searching for food. From the boulder, the two men could see the river below them. The rapids were slow there, and they couldn't hear the running water from that high up. A nearly identical cliff and forest were on the other side of the river.

Earlier, he surprised himself by being ready ten minutes before Scout's scheduled arrival at his apartment complex and had eagerly met the man in the parking lot. Since Scout hadn't asked for Alex's address, it was safe to assume he got it from the personnel files.

After leaving the Paradox that morning—and, thankfully, not running into anyone he recognized—Alex rushed home and finally breathed a sigh of relief when he entered his apartment. He spent about an hour sitting on the couch, replaying the last fourteen hours or so in his mind. Never had he suspected Scout was interested in being more than his employer or even friends with him. Had he missed some obvious clues? He doubted it. More likely, Scout just excelled at hiding his feelings. So, what had changed from yesterday afternoon to last night?

The more Alex thought about it, the happier he seemed to be about the change in direction, even though he was still in shock and wary about it. He really liked Scout—a lot—and it had nothing to do with the guy's money and everything to do with the man himself.

Scout was handsome, intelligent, and caring. He always seemed to put others before himself and just enjoyed life. When he talked about places he'd been to and exciting things he'd done, one could tell the man wasn't bragging. His face lit up as he shared his experiences, and Alex noted the same happened to others as they listened to his stories. It was as if they lived vicariously through Scout, if only for a few moments.

In addition to being a successful businessman, Scout was a bit of a philanthropist, as Alex had learned. He donated generously to a local children's hospital, an organization for women recovering from domestic abuse, and several animal rescue groups quarterly. While they were clearly tax write-offs, Alex knew that wasn't why his boss made the donations. No, Scout did it because he wanted to help make a difference in someone's or some animal's life, and he was in a position to do just that. He even spent a few three-day weekends helping to build houses for Habitat for Humanity.

All combined, the man was a very tempting package. The only things that worried Alex about what was happening between them were his job and Scout's money. Undoubtedly, some people would think that the latter was the only reason Alex was interested in the multi-millionaire, but that was so far from the truth it wasn't funny. Scout could be a waiter or a janitor, living paycheck to paycheck, and Alex would still want him.

"So, tell me about New York," Scout said after swallowing a bite of his sandwich.

"You've never been there?"

He shrugged. "Years ago—about twenty or so. It was in my teens—I know that. I mean, I've flown through JFK and LaGuardia many times, but since I never left the airport, those don't really count."

Alex chuckled. "No, that definitely doesn't count. Some people think that visiting New York City will be a breeze because they've lived in other cities, but it's a world of its own, and there's nothing else like it. I lived in a studio apartment in Tribeca, not far from the Four Seasons."

"I don't think we went there—Tribeca, I mean. I remember going to the Statue of Liberty, the Intrepid, South Street Seaport, and a few other places. We also went to see *Cats* on Broadway."

"What time of year were you there?"

Scout thought for a moment before answering. "Spring, I think. Around this time of year. Why?"

"You've got to visit Rockefeller Center sometime in

December when the big Christmas tree is up. Then, walk around, checking out some of the store displays. Some go all out, and people line up just to get close to see every little detail. It was my favorite time of the year there, as long as the temperatures didn't dip below twenty degrees."

"Maybe we could go some time, and you could show me all the sights. Stuff I missed the first time I was there."

Alex paused mid-chew, stunned by the other man's suggestion. Scout smirked at him. "I'm not looking for a brief fling with you, babe. I want to make plans with you—go places, see things, have new experiences." When Alex frowned, Scout asked, "What?"

He paused, choosing his words carefully because he didn't want to insult Scout. "If we date, I'm afraid people will think I'm only with you because of your money."

"Oh, thank God. I thought you were upset because I called you 'babe.'" Scout rolled his eyes. "Trust me when I say I've become a human bloodhound regarding people and my money. It doesn't take long before I know if it's me or my bank account a person wants to get close to. The first time we ate at that Mexican restaurant for lunch, you pulled out your wallet before I could grab mine. I watched you. You weren't making a lame attempt to pay while waiting for me to say I'd get the check. You acted like it was your turn to pay, which was no big deal—just like you'd do if you were out with your friends and family. In fact, if I were to hazard a guess, I think my money makes you more nervous than anything."

"You're so far out of my league, it isn't funny, Sc—"

"Bullshit, Alex." Anger flared in his eyes. "I'm *not* out of your league. I'm just a guy who is very interested in you and just happens to have good business sense. Like you, I was raised by a loving family who didn't mind when I came out to them. My parents taught me right from wrong, to treat everyone as if they were my equal or even better than me, and to stand up and take chances in life. And that's what I'm doing right now— well, not the standing up part, but I could do that if you really want me to, but I'm comfortable at the moment. But the taking a chance part? Yeah, that's what I'm doing. I never considered having a long-term relation- ship with someone until you came along. With the guys I've dated in the past, I always knew there would come a time when the relationship ran its course and it would be over. And I was okay with that. But with you? Damn it, with you, I don't want to see a time when you're not in my life . . . by my side . . . in my bed."

As Alex gaped at him, Scout pushed their food aside and closed the distance between them. Scout's intense stare flittered from Alex's mouth to his eyes and back again. His voice dropped to just above a whisper. "Do you remember what it was like to kiss me last night? Because I'm more than happy to remind you."

Alex groaned. While some of the night before was

still a bit of a blur, that kiss was in full focus in his mind. "I remember."

A smirk was the only response he got until Scout leaned in and kissed him. Alex's eyes fluttered shut as he tilted his head to get a better angle. While he had so many uncertainties about a relationship with Scout, they all fled his mind at the taste of the man he had dreamed about for weeks. Yeah, he remembered they kissed last night, but his recollection didn't come close to what he experienced right then.

His heart pounded against his ribcage as myriad emotions bubbled to the surface. Alex thought he'd been in love before, but now he knew those times were imitations of the real thing. What he felt for Scout was more than he ever expected to feel for anyone in his life. As Scout said earlier, Alex hated leaving work at the end of the day, especially on Fridays, with no plans for the weekend because it meant he wouldn't see his boss, his obsession for far too long.

Scout scooted closer and gently pushed on Alex's shoulders until he was flat on his back. The boulder wasn't the most comfortable thing in the world, but Alex didn't give a crap as the other man straddled him, never letting their mouths part. Their tongues clashed and fought for supremacy, but Alex knew it was a losing battle. Scout was pure alpha, and Alex was compelled to submit to him. He had always been the bottom in his relationships, and honestly, he had no desire to be the top.

They made out for a while, and Alex was grateful Scout didn't push him for more than the basic exploration he was content with. Yes, he'd fantasized about Scout for weeks now, of having dirty, mind-blowing sex with the man, but Alex wasn't ready to make that a reality yet. Scout was special, and Alex didn't want to do anything that might sideline this thing growing between them.

When Scout slowed the kiss and then gave Alex a few soft pecks on his lips before sitting upright, Alex set his hands on the other man's thighs, trying to ignore the stiff erection just a few inches above that, being restrained by faded denim.

Scout smiled down at him and caressed Alex's chest with the palms of his hands. "You know, I could kiss you for hours."

A blush stole across Alex's cheeks. "You're not so bad yourself."

Rolling off Alex, Scout adjusted himself and then got to his feet with a wince and a groan. "I promised we'd take this slowly, so I'm going to think with my big head and not my little one—although he's not so little." The man smiled smugly, and it was so sexy on him, causing Alex's cock to twitch with want and need, but he ignored it. At some point, they would take the next step—Alex was confident about that, but for now, he was content with what just happened between them.

As Scout held out his hand and helped Alex to his feet, he said, "Anyway, why don't we clean this up and take a walk? There's a waterfall up that way," he gestured to the north, "that I want to show you."

For the next two hours, they wandered around, exploring the area, pointing things out to each other, and just talking. It was precisely the first date Scout had seemed to want it to be. And if he were honest, it was the best date Alex was ever on. They both asked questions and got to know each other more personally than employer/employee. Somewhere along the way, Alex realized he was falling in love—truly in love—for the first time in his life.

Eight

The past two weeks were awesome—actually, beyond awesome, in Scout's opinion. While he and Alex agreed to keep things professional at the office, they'd gone on several more dates after hours. They wanted to keep their growing relationship between them, for now, as they got to know each other better on a personal level. Since their first date, they'd gone out to a movie, a new local art exhibit Alex wanted to check out, and bowling—something Scout hadn't done in years. Thank God he hadn't made a fool of himself by throwing nothing but gutter balls.

Until Alex, Scout never realized how most of the dates he went on in the past were expensive ones, in one way or another, usually with him footing the bill. And while Scout could easily afford to pay for everything, each time they went out, his new boyfriend refused to let him. They took turns or went Dutch, which Scout was okay with. He didn't care what they did or who paid for it as long as they were together. All that mattered was spending time with the man he was falling in love with—hopelessly, irreversibly in love with.

In addition to going out a few nights, there had been other dates when they stayed in Scout's penthouse. They enjoyed spending the evening cooking dinner together and watching TV—a movie, sports, or the latest episode of a new reality show they were both into. Scout was surprised and pleased when he learned Alex liked to play chess. Over the past six days, they tried to outwit each other on the handcrafted marble set Scout bought in Italy a few years ago. They seemed to be on the same playing level, so it was challenging to determine their next moves.

Currently, it was Scout's turn, and he was in danger of losing his queen, so he studied the checkered board whenever he got a chance over the past thirty hours. He had a feeling he was screwed and would have to suck it up and make a move soon.

During several evenings at home, Scout entertained his new boyfriend by playing the piano. One night, he discovered Alex could sing beautifully. After finding out who his favorite artists were, Scout learned many of their songs so that he could listen to the man's deep baritone voice as he sang along.

A knock on his office door drew his attention away from the advertising plans his marketing team had devised for Paradox-North in Seattle. They were just waiting for his final approval before setting it all in motion.

Delilah strode in and shut the door behind her. Sitting back in his chair, Scout waited for her to take a seat. From her amused expression, something was on her mind. "So, are you going to tell me if the rumors are true, or do I have to guess?"

"What rumors?"

"About you and Alex."

Scout groaned and rolled his eyes. He should've known someone would figure out Alex and he were dating, and once that happened, the rumor mill would run rampant. He wasn't surprised his secretary didn't beat around the bush and just asked him outright. Scout loved Delilah like an aunt, and she treated him like a nephew. And she had his back—always.

"You want to tell me exactly what the rumors are?"

"I'd rather you tell me the truth so I can collect the fifty-dollar bet I made with Sarah."

"Ah." He wasn't shocked or insulted by the two women betting on his love life. Sarah Nichols, the head of Human Resources, had worked at Turner Continental since the beginning and helped Scout grow the company from the ground up.

If the rumor mill had figured things out, there was no reason to continue hiding the fact that he and Alex were dating. Actually, it was a given that the current gossip wasn't a hundred percent accurate, so he might as well set the record straight. Scout had told Alex that, eventually, their relationship would be exposed, and he had no intention of denying it if someone asked him about it. He never hid his sexuality from anyone since he came out of the closet shortly after graduating high school.

"Alex and I are dating. It just happened, and only recently." When Delilah grinned at him, he added, "I like him, Dee. A lot. I never thought I'd find someone I wanted to spend my life with, but . . ."

"But you did, and I'm so happy for you . . . both of you. He's good for you, Scout. You've been walking around for the past two weeks happier than I can ever remember seeing you."

"I am happy. In fact, I want to introduce him to my folks next weekend."

Her eyebrows shot up. "That fast?"

"That fast."

"Damn. When you were dating that Michael idiot a few years ago, it was four or five months before you introduced him to your parents."

"And a week later, we broke up." Michael Davis, a lawyer, was one of only two boyfriends Scout had ever introduced to his family. He should've listened to his gut back then and put it off for a few more weeks. However, one of his sisters found out he was dating someone and insisted that Scout bring Michael to her engagement party. Six days afterward, Scout discovered Michael had cheated on him and told him to take a hike. The only other guy he brought home to meet his family was a guy he dated for a year in college. Things ended more amicably that time, but they'd still ended.

"Because it wasn't meant to be. I told you then I didn't think he was the right man for you."

"My mom did, too, after I told her it was over." He paused. "Do you think they'll like Alex?"

"Of course they will. What's not to like? He's smart, polite, and has a great personality. It's obvious you're in love with him, and he's in love with you. Well, at least it's obvious to me. And it will be to them too. I say, go for it."

Wow. That was the first time Delilah had ever given her stamp of approval about a man Scout dated. He was glad she had. With that, Scout made the final decision—he would take Alex to meet his parents next weekend. He'd have to check to see if his sisters could be there too.

When Alex and Scout walked into the Cock & Bull later that afternoon, many knowing smiles and looks were shot their way—especially from some of the Paradox employees. Yup, Delilah was right.

When Alex returned from running a few errands after lunch, Scout informed him the word was out about them being a couple. From the attention they garnered at the bar, it was true. Part of Alex was glad they didn't have to hide their feelings for each other anymore, but the other part was terrified about what others would think and say about the relationship. Scout had tried to assure him that the people who mattered to them would be happy for the couple. And if anyone else had a problem with the two men's relationship, they could take their opinions and shove them up their own asses. Alex wanted to agree with him, but Scout wasn't the one who'd be painted as a gold-digger by some people.

"Hey, guys. What can I get you?" Austin asked as they found seats at the bar. The place would be in full swing for happy hour in another fifteen or twenty minutes.

Scout glanced at Alex. "The usual?"

"Sounds good."

As much as he tried to act normal, Alex couldn't shake the butterflies in his gut. While he had a great time with Scout over the past two weeks, the one thing they hadn't done yet was have sex. A lot of heavy make-out sessions? Yes. Blow-jobs and rutting with many an orgasm. Yup, those too. Full-on sex? Nope. But he had a feeling that would change sometime during the weekend. Yeah, he'd asked Scout if they could take things slowly, but he was ready to take the relationship to the next level and hoped Scout was too.

A half-hour later, Scout got up and headed to the men's room as Alex talked with Gino, who had the night off from bartending. The two of them had quickly fallen back into a friendship that was now stronger than it was in high school. Through Gino, Alex also reconnected with several others from back then, and he regretted not using social media more often over the years to stay in touch with more people he went to school with. Tomorrow night, a bunch of them would gather at the Cock & Bull for an impromptu reunion that seemed to grow larger by the hour as more and more old friends found out about it. Alex looked forward to seeing his old friends again and introducing Scout to them and vice versa.

The new couple were slowly getting to know each other's friends but hadn't had the opportunity to do the same with their families. Alex hadn't even told his parents he was dating someone yet, but his sister, Amber, dragged it out of him one day while he talked to her on the phone and got distracted by Scout's fine-looking ass.

"Well, well, well. Who do we have here?" a male voice inquired just behind Alex's right ear, causing him to startle. Gino's eyes narrowed as he frowned and stared at the person behind Alex.

Turning slightly, Alex eyed the man. He didn't recognize the blue-eyed blond, who was about five feet ten with a medium build, but the guy seemed to know Alex. He was good-looking—a pretty boy—but too much so for Alex's taste. With his perfectly coifed hair, flawless skin, starched designer clothes, and manicured nails, the guy was undoubtedly high maintenance.

"Erik, what the hell are you doing here?" Gino asked.

Erik. Alex had heard that name several times since working at the Paradox. From the obnoxious sneer on the man's face, as he stared at Alex, it was a fair bet he was Scout's former assistant. The one who had an unrequited obsession with his employer and messed with Scout's personal life, causing him to fire the guy.

Ignoring Gino, Erik glared at Alex. "I hear you've been fucking Scout. Don't get too comfortable, though, bitch. He'll use you and then kick you out when you want more from him. He's done it before."

Anger coursed through Alex, and he got to his feet to square off with the other man. While he usually tried to avoid office gossip, he had heard quite a bit about Erik from other Paradox employees and Gino and Austin since he started working for Scout. None of it had been good.

It also appeared the rumor mill had Alex and Scout shagging each other, even though that hadn't happened yet.

"Look, I know who you are, and I honestly don't give a shit about anything you have to say about Scout."

"Oh, but you should, skank. You see—"

Alex made a slashing motion with his hand and narrowed his eyes. "Did you seriously just call me a skank? What are you? Fifteen? Grow the fuck up."

"That, right there . . ." Scout interrupted as he sidled in next to Alex, who glanced around to see they had acquired a rather large and rapt audience. The taut expression on Scout's face said he barely kept his ire in check. "That juvenile attitude of yours, Erik, is one of the many reasons I was never attracted to you."

Alex gritted his teeth when Erik took a seductive step toward Scout, lust filling his eyes. "But, Scout, I was willing to give you everything. I *did* give you everything. I took care of you for years. He doesn't love you like I do—he's probably just chasing after you for your money." He set a hand on Scout's crossed forearms, and Alex almost decked him. "Don't let him come between us."

Scout dropped his arms, breaking the contact with the other man. His eyes narrowed in disgust. "First of all, there is no *us*, Erik—there never was and never will be. Second, not that it's any business of yours or anyone else's, but I'm the one who pursued Alex into a relationship. He was reluctant to give in because he works for me. And he's the only man I ever worked with that I've dated. That I ever *wanted* to date. He's not greedy—he's not after my money or what I can buy him. He doesn't ask for anything other than my honesty and respect and for me to be his equal when we're not in the office. In fact . . ." He pivoted to face Alex, gazing into his surprised eyes. "It's time for me to be honest about something else. I'm in love with you, Alex. Completely and utterly in love with you."

Stunned, Alex stood there, staring at Scout, for several moments before he took two steps forward, set his hands on the man's shoulders, and leaned in and rested his forehead against Scout's. Paying no attention to everyone watching them, he swallowed hard, then softly said, "I'm sorry, but you're going to have to wait until we're alone for me to say those words back to you. The first time I say them to you, I want it to be just you and me and because the moment is right. I don't want to say it to satisfy anyone else's curiosity or prove to some asshole who can't take a fucking hint that you're mine."

"That's not why I said it, Alex." Scout's voice was just as low. "I meant every word."

"I know you did."

He tilted his head and brushed his lips against Scout's. The other man groaned and lifted his hands to clutch the sides of Alex's head before deepening the kiss. Around them, there was a roar of applause, whistles, and catcalls for them to get a room, but Alex ignored everyone except Scout. He was the only one who mattered, and later that night, Alex would show and tell Scout exactly how much he loved him too.

Nine

As soon as the elevator door shut them in, Scout pinned Alex against the back wall and crushed their mouths together. They went from zero to ninety in seconds. Hands grasped and roamed, tongues danced, and hearts pounded as the elevator headed skyward. Alex knew nothing would stop them tonight. It wouldn't be long before they were in Scout's bed, naked and pleasuring each other. They would make love for the first time, and Alex wanted to savor every moment.

He knew he'd fallen hard for Scout but was so afraid to voice those three little words. Afraid Scout didn't feel the same way. Afraid others would think he was only after Scout's money—like Erik announced to everyone. The jealous bastard was not-so-quietly escorted out of the Cock & Bull by two big bouncers after Rico advised him he was permanently banned from the establishment.

However, all of Alex's fears disappeared the moment Scout announced to everyone in the pub that he was in love with Alex. The same words almost slipped from Alex's mouth in response, but he held them back and told Scout the next best thing he could think of instead.

He wanted to say "I love you" to Scout for the first time when it was just the two of them, with no eager gazes staring at them. While it wouldn't be the first time he told a guy he loved them, it was different with Scout. More meaningful. More absolute. He realized while he may have loved a few old boyfriends, he'd never been *in* love with them. It hadn't been the forever kind of love he felt for Scout. Alex doubted he would ever love another man as much as he loved the one he was making out with in a hotel elevator.

A thought penetrated his mind, and he opened his eyes, searching where the walls met the car's ceiling. He wrenched his mouth from Scout's, gasping for air. "W-wait . . . the security cameras, Scout." The last thing he wanted was for their intimate moment to be broadcast for someone else to see.

Scout kissed along Alex's smooth jawline, which he'd shaved again before they went out earlier. His teeth nipped Alex's earlobe, sending a shiver of delight down his spine. The man drove him crazy with barely a touch. Thanks to the sensual assault, Alex was on the brink of utter insanity.

In between tonguing Alex's ear, Scout whispered, "Before we got in here . . . I disabled the camera through my phone . . . because I knew . . . I wouldn't be able to wait until we got upstairs . . . I also made sure we wouldn't stop on any other floors on the way up."

Grasping the sides of his boyfriend's shirt, Scout yanked it out from under the waistband of Alex's jeans and delved his hands under the fabric. When Scout's palms made contact with bare skin, Alex swore jolts of electricity coursed through him. His cock throbbed with want and need.

The elevator car halted, and the doors slid open. The two men didn't have to worry about running into Magnus since the actor was in Los Angeles for the next week or so.

Scout stuck his hand under Alex's belt buckle, made a fist, and practically dragged him out of the elevator toward the door to his apartment. Alex was more than happy to follow along. Within seconds, they were inside and behind a closed door, attacking each other again. Shirts, shoes, socks, jeans, and briefs were disposed of as they kissed, stumbled, bumped into things and each other, and thudded against the walls leading from the front door, through the living room, down the hall, and into Scout's bedroom.

When the back of Alex's legs hit the side of the bed, Scout gently pushed on his chest, sending him falling onto his back, breathing heavily. Letting his gaze roam Scout's naked body, Alex tried to memorize every delicious contour. The man was hot with clothes on, but without? Holy shit, he was scorching. Scout's cock was a thing of beauty too—long and thick. Alex's ass clenched as he imagined what that cock would feel like inside him.

He forced his gaze upward, and his cheeks burned when he saw Scout eyeing him just as hungrily. Scout smiled. "I love it when you blush. Never thought that would be a turn-on for me, but it is."

Climbing onto the bed, Scout straddled Alex's thighs, then bent down to nuzzle his neck. He licked and nibbled his way lower, taking a few moments to lave attention on Alex's nipples. They'd never felt as sensitive as they did then, and when Scout tugged on one with his teeth, Alex involuntarily bucked his hips.

While Scout continued downward, Alex ran his hands over as much of the other man's body as he could reach. Baby-soft skin covered lean, sinewy muscle.

Without warning, Scout opened his mouth and swiped the head of Alex's weeping cock with his tongue, drawing an agonized whimper from him. The muscles in Alex's abdomen and thighs quivered with anticipation. "Please," he whispered.

"My pleasure," Scout replied, a moment before he took Alex's shaft into his mouth and sucked hard. His beard rasped deliciously against Alex's thighs.

As much as Alex wanted to watch Scout give him a blowjob, his eyes fluttered shut, and he dropped back onto the bed as his body was bombarded with conflicting sensations, each one fighting for superiority in his mind.

Scout's head bobbed up and down, and his lips and tongue worked Alex over. His hands caressed Alex's thighs, hips, and torso. Just when Alex thought he would explode—something he didn't want to happen yet—Scout released him. Rolling off him into a sitting position, Scout opened the top drawer to his night-stand and retrieved a condom and a bottle of lube. "Turn onto your right side. I want to fuck you slow for a bit. Not sure how long I'll last, but I don't want to rush this."

Smiling, Alex did as requested, giving Scout his back as he bent his left knee and drew it up toward his chest, opening his ass for better access. Scout quickly donned the condom and drizzled some lube onto the tip. He then let a few drops fall into the crack of Alex's ass. The cool liquid flowed over his puckered hole, which, a moment later, allowed two fingers to slide inside of him. It'd been a few months since he last had sex, but he easily took Scout's fingers. Taking that monster of a cock might be a bit of a challenge, but he was more than up to it.

When Scout rubbed and stimulated Alex's prostate, he gasped and moaned. Pleasure raced through every cell of his body, but he wanted . . . no, he *needed,* more.

"Please, Scout, make love to me . . . need your cock inside me."

Even though he asked for more, Alex felt a moment of remorse when Scout pulled his fingers out, but that was almost immediately replaced by the large, bulbous head of Scout's dick. Alex forced himself to relax the muscles in his ass as Scout slowly pushed in, nearly splitting him in half. The intense burn had Alex hissing, but he thrust his hips back instead of trying to escape the invasion. "Yes! Oh, God, yes!"

When Scout's cock finally slid past the tight ring of Alex's sphincter, it lit up every nerve in his ass. He panted as Scout slowly fucked him, pulling almost all the way out before gliding back in again.

After a few moments, Scout murmured, "Can't hold back much longer. Feels too fucking good." He increased the pace, driving both of them higher and higher. Reaching around Alex's hip, he grasped Alex's throbbing erection. His lightly calloused hand pumped up and down, drawing Alex closer to the orgasm that threatened to explode.

"Come for me, baby," Scout demanded before he bit Alex's earlobe. "I need you to come because I'm almost there."

Scout squeezed Alex's cock hard, and pure ecstasy streaked through his entire body as he came in spurts in his lover's hand. His mind went completely blank for a moment, focusing only on the euphoria his body experienced. After a few more punishing thrusts, Scout plunged deep and held himself there as his own climax tore through him. He cursed as he emptied his seed into the latex barrier separating him from Alex, who wished for the day they wouldn't need the protection.

Completely spent, the two men sagged into a heap, sweating and heaving for oxygen. After a few moments, Scout slid from Alex's ass and rolled onto his back, closing his eyes as his breathing slowed.

With his heart swelling within his chest, Alex flipped onto his other side and ran his hand over the coarse hair on Scout's jaw. "Look at me." When he did, Alex continued. "I love you, Scout. I've never felt for any other man what I feel for you. I'm here for as long as you'll have me."

Turning his head, Scout kissed Alex's palm. "I guess that means you'll be here for a very long time, babe, because I have no intention of ever letting you go."

Ten

Scout checked that the small, black box was safely in the inside pocket of his winter jacket for the second, third, or twentieth time in the past hour. He and Alex spent the past three days exploring New York City. While he remembered a few places from the one and only other time he was in the Big Apple, it all felt new and exciting again, with Alex playing his personal tour guide. During the daytime, they went to many tourist attractions and did quite a bit of Christmas shopping for their families and friends.

On their first night in town, they ate dinner at the Four Seasons, where they'd reserved a hotel room, and then met up with several of Alex's former coworkers and bosses in the hotel's bar for a few hours. Last night, they went to a little cabaret type place in Greenwich Village, where a good friend of Alex's was in an improv show—it'd been a lot of fun.

Tomorrow, they had tickets for a new Broadway musical everyone seemed to rave about, including the critics. But tonight . . . tonight was what Scout had been most excited about.

The two men dated for over seven months now, and Scout had never been happier in his entire life. In a couple of hours, they'd stand with hundreds of other people in Rockefeller Center, watching the Christmas show and waiting for an eighty-two-foot-tall Norway spruce tree to be lit up for the first time. According to an article Scout read in that morning's newspaper, over 18,000 multi-colored lights would come to life with the flip of a switch. At that moment, he planned to get down on one knee and ask Alex to marry him with the platinum and diamond ring he'd had custom-made a few weeks ago. In California, his and Alex's families awaited the good news. As far as Scout knew, his boyfriend had no idea that a proposal had been in the works.

The two families joined Alex and Scout for their first Thanksgiving together a week and a half ago in their penthouse. Alex finally moved in there a few weeks earlier. Scout wanted that to happen several months ago, but instead, he gave Alex the space he needed while their relationship grew. And it wasn't as if Alex hadn't spent a lot of time there with Scout, to begin with.

Two months ago, they traveled to Seattle for the

grand opening of Paradox-North. Turner Continental threw a large celebration gala and invited local dignitaries and business owners to join them. Scout's new staff at the hotel already had the banquet halls booked solid for the next eight or nine months with dozens of weddings and other events. They'd also received many rave reviews for the events they hosted since opening. All in all, the new venue was a smashing success.

Inside the bathroom, the toilet flushed, and a few moments later, Alex emerged. He picked up his gray wool coat and put it on over a red sweater that looked amazing on him. "Ready?"

Scout forced himself not to ogle the man. If he did, they'd never get uptown in time to get a good spot by the ice-skating rink in Rockefeller Center, where the tree was located. Hundreds of people would also be there, trying to find the best vantage point to view the entertainment leading up to the big finale. Scout offered to pay for an indoor spot overlooking the event, but Alex said it was more fun being down below in the middle of it all. Scout was just glad it wasn't supposed to get too cold outside. The forecast was for light snow, with the temperature hovering around thirty-four degrees with little to no wind chill.

Patting the hidden ring box one more time, then making sure he had his phone, hotel key, and wallet, Scout gestured toward the door. Instead of getting a cab or Uber, Scout arranged for a limousine to take them wherever they wanted to go tonight and a bottle of chilled champagne to celebrate after he popped the question. "Let's go."

After they arrived at Rockefeller Center, early enough to find the perfect place to watch the festivities, Scout held Alex's hand, knowing they were meant to be. Their future was together, traveling the world and experiencing new things. Maybe, one day, they'd have some kids. They both had great paternal role models, so raising a family wasn't as scary as Scout had once thought it would be. But for now, they'd settle for the two rescued dogs waiting for them back in California. The medium-sized, mixed-breed sister and brother, Apple and Jacks, were one of the Christmas presents Scout had gotten for Alex. Their foster mom was taking care of them for Scout until Christmas Eve. He couldn't wait to surprise his lover with the two pups, but first, he had a proposal to make.

Suddenly, impatient, Scout decided not to wait until the tree was lit. Without letting go of Alex's hand, Scout reached into his pocket with his other hand and withdrew the little box. Alex's eyes widened in shock as Scout dropped to one knee, and gasps and murmurs of "aww" erupted from several people around them. But Scout only had eyes for the man he loved with all his heart. "I thought I had this whole speech prepared, but now, all I can remember are these five words: Alex, will you marry me?"

Alex just gaped at him for three or four heartbeats,

but when the corners of his mouth lifted and his eyes glistened like the snowflakes that started softly falling around them, Scout knew he had his answer. Someday soon, they'd be husband and husband.

I hope you enjoyed Scout and Alex's novella. Check out Rico's story next in Cock & Bull Book 2.

Scout's Playlist

Listen to it on Spotify: Scout's Playlist

Elton John
    "Empty Garden"
    "Someone Saved My Life Tonight"
    "Candle in the Wind"
    "Little Jeannie"

Billy Joel
    "Piano Man"
    "New York State of Mind"
    "Scenes from an Italian Restaurant"
    "You're My Home"

Carole King
    "So Far Away"
    "Beautiful"

Beethoven
"Moonlight Sonata (First Movement)"
"The Tempest (Third Movement)"
"Symphony No. 5"

Mozart
"Sonata for Piano and Violin in F"
"Fantasia in D Minor"
"Piano Sonata No. 8 in A Minor"

Jerry Lee Lewis
"Great Balls of Fire"
"Whole Lotta Shakin' Going On"

Yanni
"In the Morning Light"
"Until the Last Moment"
"The Rain Must Fall"
"One Man's Dream"

John Tesh
"Key of Love"
"Can't Live a Day"
"I Do (Cherish You)"

Nora Jones
"Come Away with Me"
"Thinking About You"

(WITH **13** OTHER AUTHORS)

Jack Be Nimble: A Trident Security-Related Short Story

***DEIMOS SERIES

Handling Haven: Special Forces: Operation Alpha

Cheating the Devil: Special Forces: Operation Alpha

TRIDENT SECURITY OMEGA TEAM SERIES

Mountain of Evil

A Dead Man's Pulse

Forty Days & One Knight

DOMS OF THE COVENANT SERIES

Double Down & Dirty

Entertaining Distraction

Knot a Chance

Finding His Forever

BLACKHAWK SECURITY SERIES

Tuff Enough

Blood Bound

MASTER KEY SERIES

Master Key Resort

Master Cordell

HAZARD FALLS SERIES

Don't Fight It

Don't Shoot the Messenger

Cock & Bull Series

Scout

Rico

Malone Brothers Series

Her Secret

Her Sleuth

Largo Ridge Series

Cold Feet

Antelope Rock Series
(co-authored with J.B. Havens)

Wannabe in Wyoming

Wistful in Wyoming

Award-Winning Standalone Books

The Road to Solace

Scattered Moments in Time: A Collection of Short Stories & More

Standalone Books

Sweet Revenge (A Novella)

The Sugarplum Fairy (A Novella)

***The Bid on Love Series

(with 7 other authors!)

Going, Going, Gone: Book 2

***The Collective: Season Two

(with 7 other authors!)

Angst: Book 7

***Special Collections

Trident Security Series: Volume I

Trident Security Series: Volume II

Trident Security Series: Volume III

Trident Security Series: Volume IV

Trident Security Series: Volume V

Trident Security Series: Volume VI

About Samantha Cole

USA Today Bestselling Author and Award-Winning Author Samantha Cole is a retired policewoman and former paramedic. Using her life experiences and training, she strives to find the perfect mix of suspense and romance for her readers to enjoy.

Awards:

Wannabe in Wyoming (co-authored by J.B. Havens) won the bronze medal in the 2021 Readers' Favorite Awards in the General Romance category.

Scattered Moments in Time, won the gold medal in the 2020 Readers' Favorite Awards in the Fiction Anthology category.

The Road to Solace (formerly *The Friar*), won the silver medal in the 2017 Readers' Favorite Awards in the Contemporary Romance category.

Samantha has over thirty-five books published throughout several different series as well as a few standalone novels. A full list can be found on her website.

Sexy Six-Pack's Sirens Group on Facebook
Website: www.samanthacoleauthor.com
Newsletter: www.geni.us/SCNews

facebook.com/SamanthaColeAuthor

instagram.com/samanthacoleauthor

bookbub.com/profile/samantha-a-cole

goodreads.com/SamanthaCole

amazon.com/Samantha-A-Cole/e/B00X53K3X8